THE WORLD IS A BANANA

Robert McCrum was born and educated in Cambridge. He is the author of three novels, *In the Secret State*, *A Loss of Heart*, and *The Fabulous Englishman*. He was the originator of the BBC television series *The Story of English* and co-author of the accompanying book (Faber and Faber 1986). *The World is a Banana* is his first full length story for children.

ff

THE WORLD IS
A BANANA

Robert McCrum

faber and faber

LONDON · BOSTON

First published in Great Britain 1988
by Hamish Hamilton Children's Books
First published in paperback in 1989
by Faber and Faber Limited
3 Queen Square London WC1N 3AU

Typeset by Goodfellow & Egan Ltd Cambridge
Printed in Great Britain by
Cox & Wyman Ltd Reading Berkshire
All rights reserved

*British Library Cataloguing in Publication Data
is available*

ISBN 0-571-15328-3

'The Llama' is taken from *I Wouldn't Have Missed It*
by Ogden Nash, by kind permission of André Deutsch.

For Nigel, Suzan, Ned, Jack and Harry

Contents

— Chapter One —

THE FLATLANDS

The trouble with Tom was that he was always dreaming about adventures. He simply couldn't help it. He was sorry, but there it was. It was as though Life with a capital L always worked out that way when it came around to Tom's bit of it. It probably didn't help that he was extremely curious about things, in fact about practically everything. He had the sort of face that has "I wonder why . . .?" written all over it. He was also, at least according to his mum, a bit of a show-off. Well, why shouldn't he have jokes on his T-shirts and stickers on his dad's car? That was his side of the story. And he was, of course, incredibly untidy.

"If you didn't talk so much," his mother would say, "you wouldn't make such a mess." The trouble was he *liked* talking. In school, he always sat with the chatterboxes at the back. On his way home he'd be discussing his idea for a new invention that would make felt pens last forever. And when he wasn't talking he was planning the best adventures in the world.

Tom lived with his mother and father and his baby sister Sarah in a village outside one of the loveliest old towns in England. The houses in the village were dotted about an open green and all around the land was as flat as a pancake. When the wind blew from the east it howled across the fields and ditches like a banshee. After dark it could be very spooky, and Tom imagined witches riding about on broomsticks putting spells on people like Mrs Grant, the fat lady in the house next door.

Just outside the village was a solitary hill that looked, Tom thought, like a sleeping monster, or perhaps a wounded monster. There was this big white scar where a cement factory was eating its way into the monster's chalky insides. Day after day, the two factory chimneys, poking above the trees beyond the green, breathed plumes of white smoke into the wide blue sky above the surrounding flatlands. The factory itself was covered in grey dust and from the village Tom could hear its machinery grinding away non-stop day and night, as if the monster was in pain.

There were people in the village who worked in the cement factory, but no one knew much about them. The security checkpoint was guarded night and day and Tom often had the feeling that there was more going on inside than people liked to admit. "What nonsense you talk," his father would say with a smile. "It's just a cement factory and that's all there is to it."

His father was a computer scientist whose job was so secret that no one was allowed to know anything about it. Tom was rather proud of the fact that his dad was special in this way, even though just occasionally it would have been nice to know, like his friends at school, where his father went to work every day, and what exactly he got up to there.

When Tom's dad was at home he was a bit of an amateur inventor, what he called "a boffin", one of Tom's favourite words. The house was full of his gadgets. There was his patent elderberry wine-making machine, his generator that ran off cow-pats and manure; there were his solar power panels made of old radiators, and worst of all there were his remote-controlled garage doors that were always getting people locked inside. But not Mrs Grant, which was the problem.

Their house was very old with beams in the walls and bumpy stone floors. Tom loved the idea of sleeping at the top of the house, under the stars. Up here he became an astronaut spinning lazily towards the moon in his spaceship. Tom was fascinated by the sky at night. He was also keen on card tricks, prehistoric monsters, the kings and queens of England, his father's video games, Top of the Pops, the West Indian cricket team, *The Guinness Book of Records*, the America's Cup, Dr Who and the A-Team. But the stars and the universe were his favourite.

Sometimes, when the night was clear, he and his father would drive out into the nearby country with a small telescope and the map of the night sky clipped out of the newspaper. The road that ran through the village went past the church with the ghostly medieval graveyard, straight over a fen causeway, past Tom's school, past the weird cement factory and up the long hill with the view over the flatlands. When it was dark they could see the lights of the village twinkling below them and beyond that the amber lights of other villages among the trees, and beyond that the glare of the town and the runway of the local airport. When the moon was full and the sky was clear, the land's horizon stretched like the edge of a knife in every direction.

Up here it was like being on the edge of the world. They would park the car in a lay-by and climb the gate into a field sloping away down the hill. Tom's father carried a torch and a compass. He would spread the map on the ground and show his son where the Evening Star always shone, explain black holes and identify the Milky Way. Tom loved it when he talked about the secrets of the universe, using strange words that he had to look up in his dictionary: constellations, quasars, supernovae, galaxies and the Crab Nebula.

For Tom it was all magic. Under the night sky, he was dumbstruck. He would stare up and up at the vast black night and try to imagine the millions of light years between the stars. Sometimes, when he was feeling happy, the stars would twinkle down at him like friends. At other times, when he was feeling blue, he would press the cold telescope to his eye and feel the icy stare of the glittering stars with a terrible feeling of fear. He once asked his father if he found the stars frightening, but his father, a practical man with a logical mind, said simply:

"The stars are suns from other galaxies. Our sun isn't frightening. So there's nothing to worry about."

They'd had a similar conversation a few months later. This time Tom's father just said: "You can trust the universe, Tom. It's always out there, all around us."

And that was that. But Tom *did* worry about the stars and what they meant and what they were saying to him. The world was full of strange wonders he didn't understand: lasers and satellite telephone calls, Cruise missiles and heart transplants – but when he looked up at the stars all of that seemed less worrying, less important. You could talk to the stars, and they gave you a kind of answer. Look at us, they said, we've been here for millions of years. Then one day he made a discovery about the stars that made him even more curious.

Usually, when he and his father drove up the long hill to look at the sky at night it was dark. They never went up the hill in the daytime. There was something about the cement factory that discouraged sightseers. Anyway, the road didn't go anywhere special and Tom's father, who was a bit of an efficiency-freak, preferred to go to the town by the direct route, the main road. The road up the hill was something special between Tom and his dad, and that was why the star-gazing trips were always a bit of an adventure. It was a Saturday in May. The cherry blossom was bursting out in the village gardens. The trees on the edge of the village green had the bright emerald leaves of early summer. That morning at breakfast, after Tom's dad had nearly set fire to the kitchen with his new gas-powered toaster, he said: "Well, I think it's a good day for a mystery drive." Tom and his mum looked at each other and groaned. They knew what that meant. Mystery drives meant motorways.

Tom's dad was not just keen on efficiency, he was crazy about new roads. Whenever a new stretch of motorway was being built, Tom's dad had to go and have a look at it, what he called "make an inspection". It was as though he was personally responsible. So they would trudge through the mud, look at half-completed flyovers, and dream about the day when the road would be finished.

Tom's mum immediately said that she had to look after the baby and do some gardening. *Thanks, mum*, thought Tom, *Thanks a lot*. There was no escape. "It'll be very interesting," said Tom's dad as they climbed into the car. "The Prime Minister is opening it next week. Perhaps we can be the first to drive along it." *Big deal*, thought Tom.

They set off. "We'll take a short cut," said his father, "and go over the hill."

It was strange going up the hill in the daylight. It seemed somehow smaller. As they began to go down the other side, Tom noticed something in the flatlands ahead he'd been wanting to discuss with his dad for ages.

"Hey! What's that, Dad?" he said suddenly, interrupting his own discussion of a plan to use the smoke from the cement factory to provide central heating for the entire village.

"What's what?" His dad seemed to have something on his mind.

"Look!" said Tom, pointing.

Away to the left, and some way off, spaced across the fen like giant open-air sculptures, was a chain of white satellite saucers.

"Hey, Dad," he said, tugging at his father's sleeve. "Just stop for a moment. I want to have a look."

"Okay," said his father, rather reluctantly. From the expression on his face, Tom knew that the white saucers were obviously to do with his dad's work – and *no one* was allowed to talk about that. Well, it was too late now. He'd just have to try and jolly him along and hope he didn't get cross.

They drove slowly down the hill. Tom was already counting. "One, two, three . . ." There were seven. *Seven for the seven stars in the sky*, Tom said to himself.

At the bottom, his father pulled over. "Wow!" said Tom. "Hey man!" he added under his breath, in his West Indian cricketer voice, "this is wicked, real wicked."

It was a hot, clear morning. The unearthly white saucers, tilting up at the sky, stretched one behind the other for perhaps a mile.

"This," said his father very matter-of-factly and as though it was the most normal thing in the world, "is what we call a radio observatory. There are some stars that are so far away they cannot be seen with the naked eye, or even by the most powerful telescope in the world. But these stars send out radio signals, very faint radio signals, and these radio telescopes can detect them."

"You mean the stars are sending messages to us?"

"Well, yes. You could put it like that."

Tom was very excited. Messages from the far side of the universe! "Can't we go and have a look?"

"Not today," said his father, with that distant tone in his voice. "We've got this motorway inspection to make. Another time."

That was his dad all over. Mr Motorway Inspection. *Oh Well* . . . At least they'd had a bit of a discussion. They drove on. The motorway was nearly finished, but apparently the public wasn't allowed to drive down it until the Prime Minister had made a speech. So Tom's dad contented himself with calculating –

map in hand, pointing like a general – how much time the new road would save and wondering whether "they" shouldn't now connect the motorway with the old by-pass. Usually when he talked about motorways, Tom could never work out why his dad hadn't got a job as a motorway planner. Today was different though, and when he thought about it afterwards he realised that on this occasion his dad's mind was on other things.

In fact they set off back home much sooner than Tom expected. Normally after such a trip he would be discussing the mysteries of cat's eyes or fog hazard lamps. But today his mind was buzzing with the radio observatory and the signals from outer space. Half of him wanted to get back home to see what his *Guinness Book of Records* had to say. The other half wanted a second look. He made his father take the same road back home. Once again they drove slowly past the strange silent line of satellite saucers, gleaming white in the sunshine.

"Is there a computer analysing these radio signals?" asked Tom.

"Most things that matter are analysed by computers these days," said his father unhelpfully.

Tom didn't give up. "And are these radio telescopes to do with your computer?"

His father didn't answer at once, but accelerated the car to the top of the hill. "One day," he said, after a lot of thought, "I'll explain everything."

"If they are connected to your computer," said Tom triumphantly, "why can't we see them properly?"

He was frowning now. "Well, perhaps we can."

Tom felt quite reckless today. "When?"

"Sometime soon." His father seemed unwilling to talk about it, except to say that he would "have to get permission".

Something was obviously wrong. As they coasted down to the village, Tom noticed that his father was wearing his irritated face. He wondered whether it was because he had asked about the computer. He decided to keep his mouth shut and not ask any more questions. Generally speaking, he trusted his dad, and he was fairly sure that the day would eventually come when they would be able to make a special investigation of the radio observatory and all its fascinating secrets.

— Chapter Two —

AN UNEXPECTED DISAPPEARANCE

But it didn't. Instead, something else happened.

A few days after the conversation about the radio observatory, Tom came home from school and saw the family car parked in front. That was good. It meant his father was home from work early. Then he noticed another car parked at the side of the house, hidden by the garage, a black BMW. He was about to run in to find out what was going on when the front door opened and his mother, accompanied by two men in raincoats, stepped out into the driveway.

Tom stopped. He stood in the shadow of a copper beech tree and watched. His mother was shaking hands with the men in the raincoats. Before he could make out their expressions, they turned, climbed into the smart black BMW, and drove slowly towards the main road. Tom opened his school satchel and took out a felt pen. Miraculously it had not run dry. Obviously, he should make a note of the number-plate. CYW D 505. "That's an odd one," he said out loud.

He waited until the black car with the two strangers had disappeared. Then he ran into the house to find his mother. She was in the kitchen, standing by the sink, looking out of the window. Suddenly he realised his heart was pounding with fear. "Hello, Mum," he said. "Where's Dad?"

Then he saw that there was someone else, a large bundle in a hideous pink overcoat, sitting on a chair in the corner, holding a glass of sherry. It was their neighbour, the big local cross-patch.

"Oh, hello, Mrs Grant," said Tom. "How are you?" It was, he felt, always worth asking this question on the off-chance that the old baggage would admit to some incurable disease.

"I'm just having a talk with Mrs Grant," his mother interrupted. "Will you go and play in the garden, please."

Now he noticed that she was holding his baby sister, Sarah, in her arms and rocking her to and fro.

"Where's Dad?" he repeated.

"He's not here just at the moment," said his mother.

"Who were those two men?" His mother looked at him blankly. "The two men in raincoats with the black BMW?" He was about to add that he had made a note of their number, but something told him not to. "Were they policemen?"

"No, Tom – " now Mrs Grant was interrupting in that horrible wheezing voice of hers – "they were not policemen, or burglars for that matter. Your mother will explain everything very soon. Now run along and play outside."

So Tom went out into the garden, thinking *silly old*

cow. His cheeks were burning with resentment. What did they think he was – a baby! *I'm ten years old. Don't double figures mean anything?* As far as he was concerned, Mrs Grant drank too much sherry, smoked too many cigarettes and bossed everybody around too much. *Bossy old cow*.

Everything seemed very still and rather strange. He took out his go-kart and began to go through his usual pit-stop routine in preparation for the next grand prix, revving the engines in his head. But he didn't feel very enthusiastic about Formula One today and he soon began wondering where his father was. If the car was here, he should be home. What were those two men in raincoats doing? Not policemen, according to Mrs Grant. *What does she know?* He walked quietly back towards the kitchen.

And then he heard the crying. It was his mother. Mrs Grant was comforting her. Tom stood outside the back door wondering whether to go in or not. It wasn't right that he was being left out. If it was to do with his dad, then he had a right to know. Mrs Grant was droning on and on. *I bet she's drunk*. One day he would get her locked in the garage for a whole morning.

He hesitated for a moment. Then very slowly he turned and went out into the garden again. *There's something wrong*, he thought, *something very wrong*. He went to the end of the small lawn. There was an old cypress sprawled over a wall. Tom and his father had built a tree house in it. He climbed up the rope ladder, pulled it after him for security and lay down on the door that served as the platform. *At least they can't get me here*, he said to himself.

He began to think. "Always look on the bright side,"

12

his dad liked to say, and would talk about something called "Optimism". His dad was good at that, looking on the bright side. And now his mum was crying. If his dad wasn't around, it would be up to him to cheer her up. *If my dad isn't around* . . . What did that mean?

He put his arm into a hole in the trunk and took out his secret supply of Fox's Glacier Mints. He lay on his back in the tree house, sucked a mint, and listened to his friends playing cricket on the village green. Overhead, a tiny single-engined aeroplane was looping the loop in a clear sky. Every time the pilot cut the engine, Tom was afraid the plane would crash and he held his breath. Now he heard his heart beating and realised he was holding his breath again. He was afraid too. *Something has happened.*

There was a cracking sound in the great rook-infested beech that towered over the cypress and the tree house. Then a familiar voice said, "Oh shit." Tom looked up. It was Harriet, the girl from the farm.

He said: "Hello, Harry." (Everybody called her Harry. She was that kind of girl.) "What are you doing up there?"

"What do you think I'm doing, numbskull? I'm stuck in this frigging tree, that's what I'm doing." That was Harry all over – as friendly as a porcupine.

Harry was an orphan, nearly two years older than Tom. She treated him like a younger brother. She lived with her uncle and aunt on the farm across the fields. Most people thought she was as tough as old boots, but Tom knew that underneath she was a big softy. He also knew that the way to her heart was teasing.

So he paid no attention to her problems with the beech tree. "How's Neddy?" he asked pleasantly.

13

Harry's uncle owned a thousand acres of good land on which he grew wheat, oats and barley. But his pride and joy was his collection of unusual farm animals. He had two Shetland ponies, a flock of Chinese geese, half a dozen Merion rams and, king of the castle, an elderly llama named Neddy. He was a gift from a friend in the circus, and it was Tom who'd christened him Neddy. For some reason he always felt especially affectionate towards him. Perhaps it was because the animal had a quiet, unruffled pride that had a strangely calming influence even on Harry, who was, as everyone said, "hyperactive". Whatever that meant.

"Listen, fatso," said Harry, "my foot's stuck in this bloody branch and you're rabbiting on about the lousy llama. Help me out of this tree and I'll give you the latest."

Tom was agile and resourceful. And he was, in fact, as thin as an eel. He scrambled out of the tree house, shinned up another rope ladder on the beech tree and swung alongside her. "What were you doing up here?"

"Minding my own business. Do get a move on."

Tom took hold of her leg and gave it a yank.

"Push, moron," she grunted, pulling her leg hard. Tom pushed and her foot came free. Slightly out of breath, they climbed down to the tree house.

"Would you like a gobstopper?" said Harry.

"Thanks." It was nice to be appreciated sometimes. Actually, Harry always compared well with adults in Tom's mind, though he could never decide whether this was because she was a girl.

"The llama," Harry announced, returning to the

14

subject, "is a pain in the bum." She began to describe its elderly, temperamental ways, its habit of spitting. But Tom was not listening. He was sucking his gobstopper and thinking about his dad. He became aware that Harry had stopped talking. "You're not listening, stink-face. I asked you a question. You're very quiet. What's the matter with you?"

Tears began to well up in Tom's eyes, but he managed to keep control. He explained what had happened.

Harry's first reaction was typical. "The men in raincoats. They must be crooks. Did you get their number?"

He nodded.

"Good. They've obviously kidnapped him," she went on. "You read about it in the newspapers all the time."

Tom pointed out that he'd seen his mother talking to the men in raincoats.

"That's the whole point. They were asking for a king's ransom. That's why she's so upset, stupid." She looked at Tom in a matter-of-fact way. "Cheer up. They'll probably have to cut off his ear before she pays up, but I expect he'll be all right in the end."

Tom looked startled. He was about to ask her what she meant when he heard his mother calling him.

"I've got to scarper," he said. "See you later."

"Don't forget to bring the car number. It may be a vital clue."

Tom scrambled out of the tree and ran to the back door. His mother was still holding Sarah, but there was no sign of Mrs Grant.

This time he knew not to ask about his dad. His

15

mother bent down and kissed him. He noticed with a shock that there were tears in her eyes still, and her face was red with crying. "Now I want you to listen carefully," she said, "and be a good boy."

Whatever else he did, he shouldn't show how worried he was. He nodded seriously.

"Daddy's gone – I mean he's had to go away for a while. He's very sorry he couldn't tell you why himself, but he asked me to explain that he's – he's all right."

His mother paused. Tom thought she might start crying again, and so he said, "It's okay, Mum," in a rather small voice.

She went on: "I don't know how long he'll have to be away, but let's hope he'll be back soon."

"Is it to do with his work?"

His mother didn't answer this at once. It was obvious that the men in raincoats hadn't given her the whole story. Then she said, "Yes, it's to do with his work. He's a very busy man, you know. He has to be away from time to time."

"Is it a conference?"

"Yes – it's a kind of conference." She paused. "He's asked me to tell you to be a good boy and pretend nothing has happened."

He thought: *If I don't ask now I never will.*

"Were those men in raincoats asking for a king's ransom? Harry says that dad must have been kid-napped."

His mother smiled for the first time. "Harry doesn't know what she's talking about. You know how she likes to make things up. You mustn't pay any attention to her."

16

He found he was almost crying too, but now he smiled bravely. "No, of course not. Harry's just silly."

His mother seemed relieved. "That's right. Just silly."

A small voice inside him said: *But not that silly*. So he asked: "Will dad be home for the solstice?" Last year, on Midsummer's Day, Tom and his father had made a special star-gazing trip up the long hill by the cement factory. This year they were planning to do it again and make it a family tradition.

"Oh, I'm sure he will be." It was obvious that his mum had no idea about the solstice, and she didn't sound very sure about what she was saying, but Tom thought it was best to try a bit of his dad's Optimism. So he said: "Well, that's okay."

His mother gave him her it's-time-to-get-ready-for-bed kiss and began putting the supper things on the table. "So everything will be just the same and Dad will be back very soon."

"That's okay," said Tom, not feeling okay about it at all.

But he did his best to be cheerful and passed on several useful bits of information from his *Guinness Book of Records* to his mum as she did the cooking. Things like the world's longest apple peel (172 feet 4 inches), the world's smelliest smell (ethyl mercaptan – a combination, apparently, of rotting cabbage, garlic, onions and sewer gas), and the fattest woman ever (Mrs Percy Pearl Washington of Milwaukee, U.S.A. who was found at her death to weigh 57 stone 2 lbs). "Almost as fat as Mrs Grant," said Tom, hoping for some kind of reaction, but his mum seemed to be lost in her thoughts.

17

Later that evening he lay in bed and looked up at the stars. He wondered if his dad (wherever he was) could see them as well. He hoped so. The stars were their secret and they were on their side. And now when he looked up at the distant constellations, and thought about the radio messages from the far side of the universe, it was as though the stars were telling him that this was the start of something very big.

Chapter Three

TOM'S VITAL CLUE

Of course things weren't the same. His mother was not her old self. Anyone could see that. You could tell she was worried, and when she said she was very busy with looking after the house and the baby, Tom knew this wasn't the whole story. Now that his dad was not there, he felt quite responsible. Almost every day another of his dad's inventions would go wrong and his mother would try to fix it and make a mess of things. Obviously it was his job to provide some of his father's magic "Optimism". So he did his best to be helpful. He carried the shopping. He hoovered the carpets. He made his bed without being asked almost every day. And he kept his own room as tidy as he could. Which was not very.

But things just weren't the same. It was as though they were pretending that everything was normal. His mother spent a lot of time at Mrs Grant's, talking things over. Tom tried to eavesdrop a couple of times but Mrs Grant had laser-sharp ears and always heard

19

him coming with an "Ah, here's Tom to see you, dear." Mrs Grant with her patronising ways was always there in the corner, a glass of sweet sherry in one hand and her packet of Rothmans in the other. She was always finding fault with him, even in front of his mum.

Silly old cow.

Worse still, they didn't go on expeditions like they used to, and worst of all his father wasn't there to discuss his ideas for inventions. But at least the weather was good. Tom spent more and more of his time out on the green and in the woods nearby, often with Harry.

The evening after his father's mysterious disappearance he had gone to look for Harry on the farm. He found her in the llama shed, mucking out.

"Hi, smell-features," she said, as he appeared.

"I've got the number – the number of the black BMW," he said.

"Give us a look, then."

He passed over the scrap of school paper. There it was: CYW D 505.

Harry screwed up her face in thought: "There's something odd about that number," she said after a moment.

Tom also knew that it was an odd number for a car, but he'd learnt a long time ago that you had to let Harry get there first if you wanted her on your side. With a real adventure like this, he definitely wanted her on his side, so he just said: "What's that, Harry?"

"Strange having the D in the middle like that. It should be at the beginning or the end." They came out of the llama shed into the sunshine. "Look," said

Harry pointing at her uncle's Volvo. "C registration – the letter comes at the beginning, not in the middle." She waved the scrap of paper in his face. "This is definitely a vital clue," she said. Tom felt pleased with himself: he'd known that from the beginning. But when she wanted to know more about the men in the raincoats he was embarrassed to say that their raincoats were just about all he could remember. "It all happened so quickly," he said apologetically. "I didn't realise what was going on until too late."

Harry was not impressed. "Moron," she said. "This is going to make my investigation a lot tougher, but I'm sure I can crack it."

For a moment, Tom was rather put out. This was supposed to be a joint adventure they were going to share together. Now Harry seemed to be taking it over for herself. That was typical. But there was no point complaining. That would only make her more determined. So instead he said: "I bet you can't solve it without my help."

"Bet you I can," said Harry, quick as a flash.

So they had a bet on it. As usual, Tom knew that Harry would never play fair if she lost. *Girls are like that*. And as usual he knew that Harriet would think him very annoying and pleased with himself if he won. *You just can't win*. He was about to ask her if she knew that the shortest place-name in the world was the French village of Y, when they heard her aunt calling her in the distance. "I'll get back to you when I've got a few leads," she said and ran off towards the farmhouse clutching the scrap of paper.

Tom turned to go home, pausing to watch Neddy the llama in the paddock on his way. He was calmly

21

chewing his dinner as usual, but somehow this did not make things any better. It only reminded him of what was missing. When they first saw the llama on Harry's farm his dad had taught him a silly rhyme:

The one-l lama,
He's a priest.
The two-ll llama,
He's a beast.
And I will bet
A silk pyjama
There isn't any
Three-lll lllama.

Tom repeated this to himself now, but it did not make him smile as it used to. It made him sad.

He climbed the stile to the public footpath. His legs were like lead. What was it his dad liked to say when Tom felt things were getting him down? "What we need is a bit of positive thinking." He was very good, his dad, at cheering everybody up with "positive thinking". Tom looked up at the sky. It was the palest blue, almost luminous, and there was the ghost of a half moon, like a tracing, above the horizon. The man in the moon didn't exist of course, but the moon's face still seemed very sad. He walked on through the summer fields of the flatlands feeling bluer and bluer.

— Chapter Four —

THE MEKON TELLS
THE TRUTH

It was an almost perfect summer that year. Morning after morning the sun rose into a clear sky over the village. Evening after evening, the flatlands' western horizon was a shepherd's delight. When June came, the long days stretched longer and longer and the shadowy hours between dusk and dawn grew so short that it seemed there was hardly any night-time at all.

Up in his cockpit under the open skylight, Tom could smell the warm night air, scented with his mother's roses, floating up from the silent garden. It became so dry that every evening she had to get out the hose and water the flowerbeds. Then Tom and his friends would take it over and fight in the water after the long hot day at school.

Almost perfect. But not quite. The one thing missing, of course, was his dad. There was no news from Harry about the mysterious car number. Tom was beginning to think that his clue was too difficult for her. But the more he thought about it, the more he didn't want to win his bet with Harry. He wanted an answer. Then one Sunday as Midsummer's Day came creeping closer, another bit of the jigsaw fell into place. This is how it happened.

It was his mother who suggested the visit to Tom's grandparents. When his dad was around this was always an adventure. Together they would plan a new and special route, preferably one that took in a newly opened stretch of motorway for his father to "make an inspection" of and approve. They would sing songs along the way and make up stories about the people in the other cars. This Sunday his mother went the quickest route she knew. But they did manage a few verses of "Poor Old Michael Finnegan" and "Green Grow the Rushes O!" just like the old days.

Nine for the nine bright shiners
Eight for the April rainers
Seven for the seven stars in the sky . . .

His grandparents were waiting for them and welcomed them in just as though everything was as usual. Tom's grandfather was tall and thin with a great bald brown head and thick glasses. Tom called him the Mekon. His grandmother was completely different, small and busy and very cosy. She was inclined to ask lots of questions. She was known as the Narg, which is Gran spelt backwards, of course. Calling her the Narg was the Mekon's idea of a joke. "How she nargs me," he would say as he lumbered off in his old slippers to feed the cat or to put another log on the fire.

The Mekon and the Narg were Tom's father's parents. His other grandparents lived in Australia. When Tom was younger, the Mekon would tease him that if he dug deep enough in the garden he would get to Australia. This was the place the Mekon called "Down Under", or sometimes "the Antipodes", which sounded suspiciously like the boring geography teacher at school.

After the usual kisses and hellos and how-are-yous, the Mekon took Tom out into the garden to show him a wall he was building. Looking back over his shoulder, Tom realised that his mother was sitting alone with the Narg in the kitchen. He could see they were talking very seriously. His mother was shaking her head a lot. After he had told the Mekon about the American who had the world record for haggis hurling, Tom decided it was time to come to the point. The thing he liked about the Mekon was that you could have a business-like conversation with him and not be treated like a child. The Mekon was always good for a few hard facts, in Tom's experience.

"Where's my dad got to, Mekon?"

But the Mekon, who was fussing with a plumb-line by the wall, didn't hear, or pretended not to, and said simply, straightening up with a grunt: "I think it's time for a spot of lunch, old boy. Shall we join the ladies?" (That was the way he liked to talk. He always made it sound very elegant and amusing.)

So Tom followed him reluctantly into the dining-room, wondering if he could trust the Mekon to give him a straight answer after all.

The lunch was a nightmare. Sarah was crying and his mother was distracted by her demands. Tom found himself being cross-questioned by the Narg about school. Was he enjoying it? What was his favourite subject? How many friends did he have? What was the head teacher like? On and on went the questions.

Tom did his best to stick to "Yes" and "No" for most of them, but every now and then his mother would say, "Come on, Tom, tell your Granny about such and such." And he would have to tell her. That was the worst of being thought a chatterbox. *This is very, very boring,* he thought to himself during a lull in the interrogation. It seemed unfair that he was expected to answer all the grown-ups' questions and not get any answers to his own. He wondered what Harry would do in this situation. Tell them all to go and jump in the lake, probably. She was always so down to earth. He wished she was with them now. Finally, when his grandmother started in on his favourite games and who was in the school team, he decided he'd had enough. He put down his knife and fork and he said:

"Look. I've had enough of these questions. I think you should tell me what's happened to my dad."

Then he burst into tears, got up, and ran out into the garden.

He went and sat by the Mekon's new wall. It was comforting to lean against the hard, warm bricks and look up at the sky. That same pale moon was up there, but this time, even though he felt miserable, it seemed to be smiling at him. He heard his father's voice on the hillside: "*You can trust the universe, Tom. It's always out there, all around us.*"

He became aware that the Mekon was standing next to him. "Listen, old son, I know you're upset, but it doesn't do your mother any good to see you fly off the handle like that."

"I don't care," said Tom.

"Cheer up, old chap. I know it seems like the end of the world, but every cloud has a silver lining."

Tom wondered if the Mekon was going to start in on the "Optimism" and "positive thinking" business, and decided that this would be more than he could stand, even from a bloke who was basically on his side. "I won't cheer up," he said stubbornly, "until I know where my dad is."

"All right," said the Mekon. "Promise you can keep a secret and I'll tell you the truth."

"I promise." (*I don't count Harry*, he said to himself.)

"Very well then," said the Mekon, settling himself on the wooden bench by the wall. "This is how it is." And he began to talk in that voice Tom loved so well.

It was all to do with science and computers, of course. Tom always knew his father was very clever with computers and now the Mekon was telling him that he also worked for the government. "And that, you see, means Secrets with a capital S."

Tom thought about this for a moment and then he remembered the conversation about the observatory and the radio messages from outer space, and how his father had seemed reluctant to talk about it. "Is it to do with the secrets of the universe, do you think?" When the Mekon looked a bit blank, he told him about the satellite saucers over the hill beyond the cement works.

The Mekon listened carefully to what he said. That was what he liked about his grandfather. He was always very considerate. Then he said, "Your father is a very clever man. So it's possible he's watching the universe as well."

"What else is he watching?"

Now the Mekon gave his grandfather's smile.

"Well, that's one of the secrets, you see. So I can't tell you – even if I knew."

Tom told him about the black BMW and the men in raincoats and wanted to know if that was a secret too. Again the Mekon smiled. "If I don't know about it, it must be." Tom was relieved that the Mekon did not seem too bothered about the men in the raincoats. *Perhaps Harry is wrong about the king's ransom.* They talked on for a while. Tom felt much better. He'd found another clue to the mystery. Now he had an idea where he might find what he was looking for. He was going to tell Harry that she'd lost the bet and that he'd found another vital clue.

The time came for them to go home. They all climbed into the family car.

"Goodbye," said the Mekon and the Narg.

"Goodbye," said Tom and his mother, waving.

The Mekon said: "Don't worry. Dad will be back soon. Everything will be okay."

Why does everyone keep on saying "Everything will be okay?" Everything was not okay, not yet. It was time to phone Harry again. "Meet me in the tree house after school," said Tom. "I've got some big news."

— Chapter Five —

HARRY IN THE
TREE HOUSE

"Hello, snot-nose. I've got some big news too," were Harriet's first words as she climbed breathlessly up the rope ladder. It was obvious she thought she'd won the bet.

"So – ?" Tom tried to appear cool. He felt cool. He was chewing some gum from the secret store in the tree.

"That car number is a government car number."

Tom chewed a bit more, the way they did on television. Then he said, trying to stay cool: "How do you know?"

"My uncle told me." She looked at Tom. "Is your dad in trouble with the government?"

Tom said: "Can you keep a secret?"

Of course she could keep a secret. "I won't even tell Neddy," she added. "And that llama knows everything."

So Tom began to explain about the secret government computers and the satellite saucers over the hill.

He explained that they were linked together. He just didn't know how or why. "That's the mystery we've got to solve," he said.

Harry listened. Finally she said, "It's very simple. You have to make contact with someone on the inside."

"On the inside?"

"Someone who's part of the organisation, brain-death. People who work with your dad. They'll know where he's being held – probably underground in a special concrete dungeon. They may even be torturing him," she added with satisfaction.

"Do you think so?"

"Very likely. They plug you into an electric toaster and burn your fingers. Or they stick lighted cigarettes into your skin. That sort of thing. I've read about it in the papers. It won't kill him," she added casually.

Tom had what his mother called "a fertile imagination", but he was also scientifically-minded. What did Harry mean when she said "They plug you into an electric toaster"? It didn't make sense. Lighted cigarettes did, though. He and Harry had stolen some of Mrs Grant's and hidden them in the tree-house for smoking on special occasions. His mind ran on to his dad again. Was he really being tortured in a concrete dungeon? He mustn't let Harry see he was worried.

Harry was still talking. " – so there's no time to lose. We've got to get inside somehow."

"You will come with me?" He was very relieved.

"Of course. This is a real adventure." Harry was beginning to make plans. "We'll go on Saturday. At the weekend the guards will be more relaxed. We'll have a better chance."

"Go where?"

"Bonehead! To the radio observatory over the hill, of course."

That was Harry at her best. A big, bold plan. A real adventure. Tom felt excited. He was about to tell her how terrific she was, when he remembered that you should never give Harry that kind of break. They began discussing the expedition and arranged to meet again in the tree house on Friday for last minute preparations.

The next day the weather broke. Thunderstorms swept across the flatlands. A bolt of lightning struck a tree in the playground and there was flooding in the road outside. The water running down the hill was chalk-white from the cement factory. Tom sat at his desk in the schoolroom listening to the rain and wondering how lightning worked. The teacher kept them in until the weather began to clear. Then he set off home, splashing through the puddles in the street. As he crossed the village green towards the house the sun came out and there was the most wonderful rainbow he had ever seen. It was a perfect arch of colour so clear and strong he felt he could stretch out his hand and touch it. His mother was coming out to meet him, pushing Sarah in the pram.

"Look, Tom," she said. "Where the rainbow ends you'll find a pot of gold."

He looked back. One end of the rainbow was plunging like a magic wand into the side of the great hill, not far from where he and his father used to watch the sky at night. He knew this was an important sign. Of course, it was the stars that you could really get messages from, but today the sky was cloudy and there was no sign even of the moon.

Later that evening, still thinking about the rainbow, he said to his mother as she tucked him up: "If I wanted to go up the hill on my own and watch the stars, I'm sure dad would let me."

His mother looked serious. "I've spoken to you about this already."

"So?" If he wasn't very careful all those sessions next door with Mrs Grant would turn his mum into a bossy old cow as well. It was up to him to keep her up to the mark. "So?" he repeated, putting on his tough face.

"You must promise me that you will never go up that hill on your own."

She was getting dangerously boring. He had to act fast to save her. He continued to be very tough. "Why?"

"Because I say so – because it's not safe."

There was a long silence. But he didn't want to hurt her too much. It was important to let her think she'd won. And anyway now he knew for sure that his father was somewhere in the radio observatory. That was the only explanation for all this bossy old cow stuff. He thought to himself: *If Harry comes. I won't be alone.* So he said, "I promise."

And just for luck, he kept his fingers crossed under the bedclothes.

— Chapter Six —

A JOURNEY
OVER THE HILL

When Friday came, Tom had a shock. There was no sign of Harriet. Nearly two years older than him, she was in a different class. He went over to her friends in the playground. "Where's Harry?" he asked.

"Where's Harry?" the girls asked each other, mimicking him. "Her boyfried wants to know."

"He can't be her boyfriend," said another girl. "He's too small."

"And too ugly."

"Go away, titch," said a third. "Harry's not here today."

He went inside and found the duty teacher. Harry's aunt had sent a message. She was not well and had to stay in bed.

Tom spent the day turning things over in his mind. The more he thought about it, the more he knew he had to carry on regardless. He had to find out what was going on inside the radio observatory. Harry's words rang in his head: "*They may even be torturing him*." She would think him very weedy if he pulled out now.

He laid his plans carefully. He borrowed some money from his best friend in class and on his way home he stopped at the village shop and bought a bag of his favourite fudge, a Crunchie and a Mars Bar.

"Midnight feasts, eh?" said Mr Jack, the village shopkeeper.

Tom knew what to do. *Behave as though everything is normal. Give nothing away.* He took his change with a smile and hid his supplies in his school satchel. Then he walked home the long way, passing the farm where Harry lived.

"Oh hello, Tom," said Harry's aunt as he came to the back door. "Harriet is in bed today. She has a temperature. I'm afraid you can't see her. She's asleep. Would you like some tea?"

Tom said no thanks, he wouldn't have tea, but would she give Harry a message. He pulled out a piece of school paper, stapled up to make an envelope, from his trouser pocket. "It's a very important message," he said.

"You are a funny boy," said Harriet's aunt. "Of course I'll give it to her."

He set off home. The llama Neddy and the other animals were grazing peacefully in the paddock. *Harry will be even sicker to miss this adventure*, he told himself, trying not to admit that he was pretty scared to be going alone.

He and Harry had taken the path across the fields a thousand times. They knew it backwards. It was good to chew things over together as you walked along. But now he was all alone. What was going to happen on

34

the expedition to the observatory? This thinking-about-the-unknown was what it must be like to be an astronaut going up into space. Looking at it that way made him feel better, and a little bit braver.

When he reached home, he found his mother in the garden, weeding the rose bed. The baby was in her pram under the willow tree. Tom went very quietly into the kitchen and took first one and then a second can of Coca-Cola from the larder. He looked out of the window. His mother was still on her hands and knees. He went quickly back to the fridge and took out a Scotch egg wrapped in cellophane paper. Next he lifted two apples from the fruitbowl. Hoping his mother wouldn't miss anything, he put everything in his satchel, including a half-empty packet of Rothmans left behind by Mrs Grant. Then he climbed up to his bedroom in the attic and hid his satchel under the bed. Finally, he went to his cupboard and took out his CRAZY BUT NOT OBNOXIOUS T-shirt. It seemed the right one for the expedition. Everything was ready.

When he came downstairs for the evening meal, he found his mother with her head in the fridge. "That's odd," she was saying, "I could swear there were two Scotch eggs here?" she looked at Tom. "Have you been helping yourself to my larder?" she asked, smiling wickedly. He blushed. "No, mum." He knew she could tell he was lying. "I mean yes," he said. Thinking quickly, he added. "I was hungry after school." She laughed and kissed him. "I hope you haven't spoilt your appetite."

Phew! That was a near one.

After supper he sat and watched the news and then

the weather forecast with special interest. It was raining in Scotland and misty in the South-West. There were thunderstorms in the Channel. But the eastern half of the country was dry and tomorrow promised to be a fine day.

He said goodnight to his mother, giving her a special kiss. He had given her a promise about not going over the hill, but only sort of. After all he *had* crossed his fingers. If he found out what had happened to his dad she'd be pleased. (As far as he could see, the men in raincoats were keeping her in the dark about that.) So he told himself it was all in a good cause.

He went upstairs to his attic bedroom. His supplies were still safe under the bed. He turned out the light and climbed under the duvet. He lay looking up at the night sky, wondering when it was safe to set off. Just in case, he set the alarm for two o'clock. He was sure he wouldn't oversleep, but you never could tell. He heard his mother pottering about, preparing for bed. The phone rang, and he heard her talking to the Mekon. Then he heard her coming upstairs. He began to doze. Suddenly he came to with a start. The alarm was ringing. It was two o'clock.

He had gone to bed half-dressed, so now he quickly pulled on his shoes and sweater and picked up the satchel with the food and the Coca-Cola. Then he crept down the stairs and into the kitchen, as quiet as a mouse. He was afraid that every footstep would wake his mother. He expected to hear her call out his name at every creak, but he made it downstairs safely. The house was still. He propped a message on the kitchen table explaining that he would be back in the evening. Then he took his anorak from behind the door and stepped quietly outside.

The village was wrapped in summer darkness, the shadowy hours before dawn. The air was still and cool. In the distance, a church bell chimed. One. Two. The sky was clear, but there was no moon. Tom walked by the friendly light of the stars, feeling incredibly excited.

He made his way along a back route he and Harry often used, avoiding the main road. Soon he was behind the parish church and the road past the cement factory towards the hill was just two hedges away.

He had met no one. He climbed a stone wall covered with ivy and dropped into the graveyard. The parish priest was old and lame and his church was falling into disrepair. The graves were smothered in weeds. One of the older tombstones, near the lych-gate, had a skull and crossbones. Tom always passed it on his way to school with a kind of awed fascination. In the darkness it was very spooky. He didn't want to run into any ghosts just now, thank you very much. He hurried through the wet grass, not looking behind him, scrambled over another wall and then he was on the road again.

As he jumped down, he looked up ahead towards the hill. The trees on the ridge were silhouetted against the sky. A strange white light was shining through the branches. For a moment he wondered what it was. Then he realised he was watching the moon rise over the hillside, bathing the flatlands in a soft grey light. The way forward stretched straight as a ruler in front of him. If his eyes followed the telephone wires he could see where it began to climb the hill. He and his father always drove along here. Now that he was on foot it seemed a vast distance. He began to walk.

It was not yet three, but away to the east the first light was creeping over the horizon. He was getting quite hot under his anorak. After half an hour, Tom reached the cement factory. It was more like a monster than ever. The chimneys were smoking away as usual. The sodium lights glared like yellow eyes in the darkness. Close to, he could hear the grinding of the cement-making machinery. Three or four huge orange cement lorries were parked next to a long grey chute, but there was no sign of life. Even the gate-house seemed deserted, though he was sure there were security men sitting behind the wire-netting. Perhaps they were watching him now. He hurried on.

He looked at his watch. Ten past three. Time was passing quicker than he expected. Baby Sarah could wake up any time now and his mother could discover that he was gone. *Will she set out and look for me in the car?* he thought. He hoped she would find his note when she went to boil Sarah's milk. He hoped she would trust him to return when he said he would. *What will happen if she comes after me?* But then he thought: *I could have gone in any direction.* Perhaps she would try this road first. She'd already said he was not to go over the hill. So he quickened his pace again, and every few steps he looked over his shoulder to check that the road was clear and no one was following.

In the moonlight, he thought every shadow on the road was a car. Then he saw a light among the trees. It was moving, whatever it was, moving fast towards him. Quick! He had to hide. He scrabbled his way up the low bank at the side of the road and tumbled into the ditch.

The car shot by. Tom kept his head down, crouching in the slime, until it had gone well past. When he poked his head out he saw that it was not his mother but Mr Jack's van going to collect the vegetables from market. He brushed the mud off his trousers, got back on to the road and began to walk again, singing to himself as he did so to keep his spirits up.

At the foot of the hill there was a sign he had never noticed before: PUBLIC FOOTPATH TO ——— 3 MILES. He knew that the radio observatory was on the edge of ———. If he took this path it would be easy once he got nearer to break off and explore. Anything that took him away from the main road was a good idea. *Perhaps*, he thought, *there will be fewer guards if I approach the observatory from the footpath*. So he turned off the road by the sign, feeling rather brave.

Tom climbed the stile and at once found himself walking through shoulder-high cow parsley. He couldn't see in the darkness, but he thought he could hear a small stream next to the path. It was very quiet. At the next stile he looked at his watch again and decided to have a rest. It was already almost four o'clock. He munched his first apple. *It's a great shame Harry isn't here.* It would have been nice to have someone to talk to and discuss the route with. Suddenly, there was a beating of wings and a loud shriek. Tom jumped in fright as an owl flew out of the trees. He looked about to see what had disturbed it. But the bird had gone and there was an eerie stillness again, broken only by the cracking of twigs and the rustling of the undergrowth as the short night passed and the countryside began to wake up.

He set off again. Now the track was beginning to wind slowly up the hill. He could feel the sweat running down his arm. His feet were aching and the satchel which had seemed light enough when he set out now weighed a ton. He struggled on. The path was not much used. In many places it was overgrown. Tom had to crawl under briars and push through patches of stinging nettles. Now and then he had to climb over a fallen tree. He felt grateful for the moonlight.

He pushed on, up and up. Finally, quite out of breath, he reached the top of the hill. He knew he was only a few hundred yards away from the main road and the view that felt like the edge of the world. From time to time he could hear early morning cars in the distance. But best of all, away to the left, and below him on the flatlands, were the satellite saucers of the radio observatory reflecting the light of the full moon.

At last, he said to himself, at last! In his excitement he began to run down the hill, his satchel thumping on his back. He wanted to get to the strange, forbidden place. He was convinced his father was in there somewhere. Harry's words echoed in his mind as he ran: "*They plug you into an electric toaster and they burn your fingers with lighted cigarettes.*" Cigarettes, cigarettes, cigarettes: he was running so hard that he missed the branch across the track, tripped and fell headlong with a thump.

The world did a somersault and he found himself sitting on the path with a painful scratch along his calf. He felt sick. For a minute or two he did not move. *This is crazy. I should never have come out on my own.* He wished Harry was with him to cheer him up. Suddenly, he wanted to be home with his mother, being made a fuss of. He was actually about to cry but then his determination came back. *It's only a scratch. I must keep going.* He tied one of the handkerchiefs he'd brought with him around the wound, and set off again, limping slightly.

The path twisted and turned. It was downhill all the way now, but he had been walking for nearly three hours and was tired. Then the land levelled out and he was on the flatland itself, walking through an avenue of beech trees. It was the magic hour before sunrise, cool and silent. The grey beech trunks were like the pillars of the Norman cathedral on the wall-poster at school, soaring up into a speckled roof of leaves and early morning light overhead. There were rooks nesting high above him, going caw-caw-caw. The beech mast crunched underfoot as he walked down the long avenue. He wondered who had planted it and how long ago.

A bit further on there was a wrecked car. All its insides had been stripped away long ago. It was just the skeleton of an old Volkswagen. Someone had obviously been camping in what was once the back seat. He felt afraid. His mother had warned him about tramps, strange men living rough in the flatlands. And then there were the witches from the fens. He looked about nervously, but the beechwood was quiet. Only the rustling of the leaves and the croaking of the rooks broke the stillness. Tom hurried on, anxious to get out into the open again.

Suddenly there was a rat-tat-tat-tat echoing across the flatlands in the blue dawn. There was no mistaking the sound. Gunfire. He stopped to listen. There

41

it was again. A crack and a whine in the half-light. He thought he could hear someone shouting. It must be the guards, practising. He began to move forward again, keeping his eyes open, very alert.

He reached a field. The cow parsley was taller than ever. He could hardly see his way forward on the path. Now the occasional burst of gunfire seemed further away. Then he caught a glimpse of a white satellite saucer, much bigger than he expected, just one field away. He pushed through the undergrowth and then his path was blocked. Right in front of him was this wire fence and on it a notice: ———— RADIO OBSERVATORY. STRICTLY PRIVATE. TRESPASSERS WILL BE PROSECUTED.

He looked at this for a while. So here he was at last. Journey's end. Of course it's private, he said to himself, there's some very expensive equipment in there. You can't have people walking in and out just like that. The boffins have got to have peace and quiet for their experiments. And you don't want people interrupting just as you are plugging someone into an electric toaster. The guards! He came to with a start. Where are the guards?

He approached the fence gingerly through the long wet grass. It was bound to be electrified. Close to, he saw it was incredibly rusty with many gaping holes. It didn't *look* electrified. He put out a finger and touched it quickly. No shock. He tried again, for longer. Still no shock. He looked up and down the wire. There was no one in sight, no guards, no nothing. *Well, here goes*, he said to himself, taking a deep breath. And he scrambled through on to the other side.

— Chapter Seven —

INTO THE RADIO
OBSERVATORY

Tom pushed through the high grass and all at once he
found himself standing on a kind of railway track.
Then he got another surprise. Just a hundred yards
away, further down the track, was an enormous satellite saucer pointing up into the sky. He looked about
him. He was alone. Stepping over the sleepers, he
picked his way towards it until he was standing in its
shadow. Close to, it was even bigger and stranger,
blotting out the early morning sun. All he could hear
was this faint metallic hum. The machinery was
obviously all switched on and ready to receive the
messages from outer space.

"Wow," he said, under his breath. His heart was
beating with fear and excitement. This was it.

Tom sat down in the grass, just off the track, and
gazed up at the saucer to see if it was moving. He
watched and watched, but it remained – or seemed to
remain – quite stationary. He followed the line of the
track with his eye. About two hundred yards away

there was another saucer, and beyond that a third, and beyond that a fourth – a line of seven, all staring at the sky.

After a while he got up. Keeping an eye out for the guards he walked down the track. The next satellite saucer was identical to the first, though it was pointing to a slightly different part of the heavens. It, too, seemed motionless. He walked on to the next one.

He was also keeping a sharp eye out for where they might be keeping his dad. Each saucer had a flight of iron steps running up into the middle of it, but there was nowhere big enough to hide anyone. And anyway there weren't any guards. The place seemed deserted. Harry's words came back to him: "*He's probably underground in a special concrete dungeon.*" He looked about. But there was no sign of any concrete dungeon nor even any tell-tale air-vents.

Suddenly he heard a car. Just in the nick of time he dived for cover in the long grass. A jeep with two men in white overalls came rattling past. They were talking and laughing. Tom was curious that the guards should be so relaxed and carefree. Perhaps they were boffins not guards. Boffins were bound to be happy in their work. "Job satisfaction" – that was the phrase his dad always used. He wondered what "job satisfaction" for the guards would mean. Lots of interesting torturing, probably.

Tom waited until the sound of the jeep had died away. Then he carried on down the track. He reached the fifth, the sixth and finally the seventh radio telescope. But he found no clues about his father. It was all very odd.

When he came to the last saucer the track ran out.

Beyond was a dirt road. In the distance he could see a collection of huts. *That must be where the men in white overalls came from* he said to himself. *And that must be where they are keeping my dad.* He looked at his watch. It was just after eight o'clock. Before he made his approach to the huts (he hadn't yet made up his mind how to do this) it was time to have his Scotch egg for breakfast.

Now that he had actually arrived at his destination, he was beginning to feel tired, and also slightly unsure about what to do next. It wouldn't do any harm to have a bit of a rest, perhaps smoke one of Mrs Grant's cigarettes, gather his strength and plan the next move. So he spread his anorak out as best he could and lay down in the long grass well out of sight. And very soon he was fast asleep.

He had hardly closed his eyes when he discovered that his mum had called out the police. She was hurrying down the hill towards him, followed by Mrs Grant and two black squad cars with sirens. Then a voice said: "Tom". He turned round and there was his dad, just as he remembered him, standing by one of the satellite saucers. Before he could say "Mrs Grant is a bossy old cow," he and his dad were underground in a secret tunnel and running for all they were worth. His mum was shouting Stop! Stop! Stop! He knew he should wait for his mother. He hesitated. His dad was laughing and laughing and laughing . . . and a voice, apparently from several miles above him, was saying "Well, look what we have here." Then his dad was nowhere to be seen and the voice, now much closer, said, "Crazy but not obnoxious, eh?"

Tom came to with a start and jumped up. Rubbing

his eyes, he found himself staring at the *longest* pair of legs. Working upwards, he passed from the faded jeans to a check shirt, to a loose tie, to the oddest, shaggiest, most lop-sided face he had ever seen. A human scarecrow, covered in sweat, brushing its straggly blonde hair out of its eyes, and peering at him through a pair of serious-looking glasses.

Tom was terrified. This was obviously one of the guards. Just because he was smiling it didn't mean he couldn't plug you into an electric toaster at a moment's notice. In fact, that smile was a dead giveaway. He was obviously looking forward to a bit of torturing.

He decided to be brave about it. "I expect you want to get on with the torture," he said, in a very matter of fact sort of way. "But could I just say hello to my dad first?"

"Come again, squire?" said the scarecrow. He wasn't exactly smiling, but he looked puzzled and friendly. He looked, at second glance, a bit like one of the trolls in Tom's fairy-tale book. But a nice troll, one you'd probably want to invite home for a game of "Trivial Pursuit".

Tom was beginning to have doubts. "You are one of the torturers, aren't you?" (On third glance, it was a very *kind* face. Perhaps he was just a part-time guard, not a torturer.)

"Torturers ?" The troll looked thoughtful. "I don't get your drift, mate. I do in-depth interviews, if that's what you mean."

"You don't have to tell me exactly where he is, but is he okay?"

The troll looked totally confused. "Steady on, old

fellow, you're going too quick for me. Who's *he* – when he's at home?"

"My dad, of course," said Tom simply.

"Oh. Of course." The troll thought for a moment, then he sat down on the grass, crossed his immensely long legs and patted the space next to him. "I think you and I have got to have a little talk." And he said it so nicely that Tom sat down next to him, quite relaxed, and began sucking a grass.

"Now then," the troll went on, "first things first. What's your name?"

"Tom."

"Where do you live, Tom?"

He pointed. "In the village over the hill. I walked here," he added proudly.

Tom was glad that the scarecrow/guard/troll/torturer/whatever seemed quite impressed. "That's quite a step for a small chap," he said. "How long have you been here?"

"An hour or so." Tom tried to sound casual about it. "I came here overnight," he said. "By the light of the moon."

"Did you indeed? Well, well, well," the troll was taking this all in. "Pleased to meet you." He stuck his hand out. "Nigel" he said.

This was not what Tom had been expecting. "Are you a torturer or a guard or a boffin?" he asked.

Nigel laughed. "Oh, none of the above, I'm afraid. I'm just a reporter, a humble hack. I'm writing a story about the radio observatory for the local paper."

Tom was pleased. Reporters always knew the inside story. "Well," he said, "perhaps they haven't told you where he's being tortured. But he is, you know. Being tortured, I mean."

"Now I was coming to that," said Nigel. "To tell you the truth I haven't the faintest idea what you are talking about."

So Tom explained everything, as clearly as he could. Occasionally Nigel would ask a question just to get things straight in his mind. He told him about his father and the two men in raincoats, and about Harry and the car number and her ideas about the guards and the torturing. He even told Nigel about things that weren't strictly to do with the situation, like about his mum and Sarah, horrible Mrs Grant and Neddy the llama and about the really interesting fact that an American called Charles Osborne had hiccoughed continuously for sixty years. Nigel was the sort of person you wanted to tell things to. "And so then, you see," Tom concluded, "I knew I had to come here and find out what was going on."

"Quite right too," said Nigel warmly. "It's obvious that we've got to get to the bottom of things."

Tom nodded. He liked the sound of "we". He felt better already. (He felt sure that if he suggested to him that it was a good idea to lock Mrs Grant in the garage Nigel would agree.) Finding Nigel was obviously a vital bit of the jigsaw. Okay, there didn't seem to be much sign of his dad, but having Nigel on the case was definitely a step in the right direction. There were still so many things he didn't understand. He told Nigel this.

Now it was Nigel's turn to do some explaining. Things were not quite as they seemed. The radio telescopes were simply radio telescopes. The huts at the end of the railway track were simply offices for the boffins who worked the equipment. And there were – he was afraid to say – no guards and no torturing.

"But what about the gunfire?" asked Tom. "Isn't that to do with the guards?"

Nigel looked thoughtful. "Oh – I see. You mean the rifle range over there?" He pointed. In the distance Tom could see a red flag flying. Nigel smiled. "That's the army." He became confidential. "Listen, Tom. We've certainly got a story to investigate, but you're barking up the wrong tree."

Tom looked disappointed.

"Cheer up," said Nigel, "The adventure's hardly begun. The mystery of your missing dad is the really important thing. That's what we have got to get to the bottom of," he said again. He got to his feet. "It's distinctly fishy, this disappearing business." He began to sound very practical. "Now from what you've told me, it sounds as though your dad runs the sister organisation of this outfit on the other side of town. It shouldn't be difficult for me to make a few inquiries." He picked up Tom's satchel. "Come along. This is where my press pass comes in rather handy. It's time for the guided tour. Just to prove there are no torture chambers."

They approached the huts. Nigel seemed to be a familiar figure about the place. He was greeted warmly and people asked him how his article was going. No one challenged Tom. "Well, here we are," said Nigel as they reached the main entrance. "Welcome to the funny farm." It was dark and cool inside after the morning sun. Tom took a while to adjust his eyes to the light. Gradually he made things out. At the far end of the hut was a huge blue chart with thousands of little white dots shining like jewels.

"This," said Nigel, "is an interstellar tracking station. This is where the astronomers here watch the sky you cannot see, the invisible universe. This is where they discover quasars and supernovae –"

"I know all about quasars," Tom broke in. "My dad told me."

"He sounds like a good bloke, your dad."

"He is," said Tom proudly. "You'd like him." He was sure his dad would like Nigel. For a start, Nigel was obviously into "positive thinking". Perhaps he was even interested in motorways, though Tom rather hoped he wasn't.

Nigel picked up a photograph from one of the desks. "Look at this," he said. "This is more than five hundred million light years from Earth. It's a radio picture."

"Where do the radio waves come from?"

"That's the energy of outer space. Thousands of tiny signals from the edge of the universe."

"You mean actual recorded messages from the other side of the universe?" said Tom. He'd believed his dad about this, of course, but now here was the evidence. It seemed a good time to tell Nigel that some stars were fourteen million light years from the planet Earth. Tom was proud of this information and hoped to impress his new friend.

Instead Nigel suddenly became down-to-earth. "Now let's face it, mate, you're a pretty long way from home yourself." He looked keenly at Tom. "Does your mother know what you've been getting up to?"

"Er, not exactly," Tom stammered. "But I said I'd be home by tea time. She'll be all right."

"I've got a feeling that she'll be worrying herself to death about you, young fellow." He steered Tom towards the door of the interstellar tracking station. "I think we'll take a ride in Apollo Thirteen before things get out of hand." He grabbed Tom by the arm. "Come along."

"But what about my dad?"

"That's why we have to get a move on. There's no time to lose. The trail could go cold at any time."

How funny, Tom thought, that he should find himself trusting this human scarecrow with straw coloured hair and jeans with holes in to help him find his dad. But that was how it was. Well, he thought, it all goes to show that you just can't judge from appearances. "Do you think we'll find him soon?" he asked.

"Soon? What's soon? Everything is relative. We'll see what we can do."

Nigel was the first grown-up who didn't say that everything was okay. Tom felt immensely relieved.

After the dark hut, it was bright in the sunshine. Tom blinked. Then he found himself sitting next to Nigel in his old landrover, Apollo Thirteen, and soon they were bouncing over the potholes towards the main road. They passed the jeep with the two men in white overalls Tom had seen before. Nigel waved and the men waved back.

"Who are they?"

"Engineers."

So much for the guards. He couldn't wait to tell Harry.

Apollo Thirteen struggled up the hill by the cement

51

factory. From up here, Tom could see how far back the huge works stretched into the quarry. The men working there were like toys next to the grey mountains of cement. Whatever his dad said, there was something about it he didn't fully understand. He was about to discuss this with Nigel when they turned a corner and there, below them, was Tom's village. It looked different in the daylight, and somehow smaller. After the adventures of his walk, it seemed no distance at all. They cruised down past the church and Nigel parked on the village green.

"Now then, Tom, you run along home." Nigel stuck out his hand. "It's been a pleasure. See you again soon."

"But what –? How will you tell me about my dad?"

"Oh, don't you worry about that."

Phone number. I must get his phone number. Harry will kill me if I don't get a phone number.

"What's your phone number?" he said out loud.

Nigel tore a sheet of paper out of his notebook and scribbled down a number. "There you are. Just ask for the ace reporter. Now don't you worry about a thing." He winked. "We'll get your dad back."

Tom jumped out of the landrover and watched it rattle noisily back up the hill towards the radio observatory. Then he turned and walked slowly, with aching feet, towards the house on the green. It was time to face up to his mum.

—— Chapter Eight ——

WHAT HIS MUM SAID

Afterwards, as he lay on his bed turning the pages of *The Guinness Book of Records* (Longest Sermon: 120 hours; Longest Prison Sentence: 10,000 years) Tom realised that she was bound to be furious with him. Mothers were like that. He had tried to explain, but it was no use, of course. When she saw that his leg was cut and bleeding, this was simply the last straw. She had spent the day frantic with worry, she said, and now she was merely angry. Tom felt about two inches high. He was very sorry to have made her so unhappy, but whatever way he looked at it he couldn't see that he'd had a choice.

She had told him to take a bath, then washed the wound and put ointment on it, and thrown his clothes, dirty and torn from his adventure, into the washing-machine. Then she had sent him upstairs to his room with what she called "a piece of her mind".

It was this "piece of her mind" that Tom was brooding on now. It all seemed rather unfair. He had tried to tell her about Nigel, the human scarecrow, but she was not interested. He had tried to explain that his father wasn't being held in an underground torture chamber at the radio observatory, but she would not listen. Brushing his explanations aside, she had talked instead about the "dangers" of "strange men", and the police who would want to arrest him for "trespassing". Finally, as a last word on the subject, she had said, "Your father is perfectly all right, Tom. He'll be home very soon."

Which he knew was a lie. He thought: *When my dad comes back* . . . It was more like an "if" than a "when", but you had to start somewhere. That was what "positive thinking" was all about. He had to assume Nigel *was* going to help, get him back. So when/if his dad came back Tom made a special resolution to ask him about all the lies he'd been told recently. Adults were always very big on telling the truth, it seemed to him, until it suited them not to. Perhaps he shouldn't wait for his dad, he should ask his mum. But that would mean giving away that he knew she wasn't telling the truth, and he thought this would upset her. He didn't want her to get more bent out of shape than she was already. When you got right down to it, she was his mum, after all.

Actually, he didn't really blame her for being cross with him. After all, she *was* all alone and it *was* his job to "behave responsibly", as she put it. What got up his nose was the fact that although he was obviously much more grown up now that his dad was away, she was still treating him like, well, like not his age. That was the problem. He decided he would have to talk this over with her tomorrow morning.

As he ran through the events of the day in his mind, he realised he couldn't wait to tell Harry about his adventures. He was sure she was going to be green with envy. At least he hoped so. That made him feel better already. And quite soon, because he was actually very tired, he fell asleep.

It was still dark when he woke up with a start. *Nigel's telephone number!* In the excitement of coming home he had forgotten all about it. He tried to remember his return. He'd stuffed the scrap of paper into his trousers and . . . his mother had put them in the washing machine! Normally, she would have turned out his pockets first, but perhaps . . . . He lay there wondering what to do. He was unable to sleep for worry. Finally he got up and went creak, creak, creak, down the stairs into the kitchen.

It was quite dark but he found the torch by the back door and flashed it into the machine. His clothes were still inside in a damp tangle. Gingerly he opened the door and began to tug his wet jeans free. He put his hand first into the front and then into the back pockets. Yes! She'd been in such a bad mood she'd just thrown the clothes into the machine and slammed the door. He closed the soggy scrap of paper in his fist, pushed the jeans back, clicked the door shut and climbed back up to his bedroom.

His bedside light seemed bright in the darkness. He straightened the paper. Despite the washing, the numbers in Nigel's handwriting were not badly smudged. Seven Seven One Six Three Five.

Nothing could be left to chance. He imagined what Harriet would say if he made a mess of things now. *Moron! Cretin! Dope! Puke-face . . . !* He took out one of his felt pens and wrote the number on the underneath of his bedside table for extra security. Then he hid Nigel's scrap of paper in a book about the World Cup.

And then he fell asleep.

When he woke, there was only one thing on his mind. How to contact Nigel again. Nigel had said, "*Don't worry about a thing*", but Tom knew that this business was too important to be left to chance. It was obvious that his mother knew nothing about what was really happening. Okay, Nigel looked like a human scarecrow, but he had the right ideas about finding his dad. He decided he would wait until his mother took the baby out shopping. Then he would phone Nigel.

But his mother had other plans. Once breakfast was over, she announced they were all going shopping.

"But *Mum!*" said Tom, panicking. "We don't normally go shopping like this."

"And *you* don't normally go walkabout. I'm not having you roaming off on your own again," she said with a smile. Tom was glad about the smile: she had obviously decided to forgive him for his adventure. Even if she wasn't about to forget it.

He had been going to raise the subject of his age and how he expected to be treated as at least ten these days, but his mum's smile was a big enough victory for one day. Perhaps if he was very good, she'd let him off the shopping expedition. So he made his bed without being asked and even volunteered to clear away the breakfast.

That turned out to be a big miscalculation. There was no way out. They were all going shopping and that was that. No argument. He began thinking up ways of escape. Mrs Grant was in the supermarket as well, stocking up on sherry and cigarettes. As usual she was very bossy. Tom mananged to bump into her trolley by-mistake-on-purpose at least once. He had read that a Frenchman, Monsieur Mangetout, had once eaten a supermarket trolley in four-and-a-half days, but now was definitely not the time to pass on this information to anyone. His mind was working overtime. He would load his trolley with Heinz 57 soup cans, block the aisle, slip past the check-out and into the pedestrian precinct. They would pursue him of course, the manager and the store detective. He'd have to run, slip down a back alley, hijack a car at gun-point probably and shake off the police, perhaps taking Mrs Grant hostage and torturing her with an electric toaster in the process . . .

"Tom." It was his mother. "You haven't been listening to a word I've said."

"Sorry, Mum."

"Now please help Mrs Grant with her basket."

Oh, Mum! Give me a break!

His mind went on buzzing. How could he get in touch with Nigel? After shopping they went to the park to show Sarah the ducks. Tom couldn't believe it. *I'm ten years old and I'm still feeding the ducks with my baby sister! What would Harry say?*

When they came back his mother made it clear that he was expected to stay in the garden where she could keep an eye on him. Tom realised with a sinking feeling that he was a prisoner in his own home. There was no way he could call Nigel and he couldn't imagine what his mother would say if Nigel phoned. *Declare World War Three probably.* He lay on the grass in the garden, staring up at the sky and praying that Nigel wouldn't ring and get his head bitten off.

Then he had a brainwave.

"Hey, Mum," he said casually at lunchtime. "Can I take some books and things to Harry's? She's in bed with flu, you know."

His mother looked very doubtful. Then she went to the telephone. "Mrs Bell? Hello . . . yes, thank you . . . yes, he turned up in the end . . . yes, I know . . . *very* dangerous . . . yes he says he wants to come and give Harriet some books and games. Will that be all right? yes . . . yes . . . you can expect him in the next half hour . . . He's just going to help me with the washing-up."

Blimey! thought Tom, as he set out through the village, *is this Colditz or what?*

Just before he came to the fields, he had to pass Mrs Grant's house. She was busy putting out her black plastic rubbish bags for the dustman. *I bet they are full of sherry bottles and fag-ends.* But as usual he just said: "Hello, Mrs Grant. How are you today?" in a fairly friendly way.

Mrs Grant looked up, very red in the face. "Now you," she said in her rasping, wheezy voice, "are a very naughty boy."

Tom was amazed. He stood there while she went on and on about how he had made his mother "sick with worry", and how his mum "had enough on her mind without you adding to her troubles". She came towards him, looking really horrible. "If I had a son who was as disobedient as you," she said, "I'd give him a good beating."

He stepped back, muttered something about it

58

being a good job she hadn't, and ran down the road towards the fields. It was so unfair! At least he was trying to do something about finding his dad. *One of these days, Mrs Grant, you've really got it coming to you.* In his mind he ran over the current Top Ten of possible fatal illnesses: *Legionnaires Disease, Rabies, Mixamytosis, Black Death, Bengal Rot, Botulism, Montezuma's Revenge, French fever, Bubonic plague . . .*

By the time he reached the llama he was feeling much better.

"Hello, Neddy," he said pleasantly.

The llama gave him a sort of llama-ish smile and, as usual, Tom reached Harry's farm in a good mood.

He found Harry sitting up in bed looking perfectly okay. "Hello, stinkface," she said cheerfully, as Mrs Bell showed Tom into the room.

"Harriet," said her aunt sternly. "I've warned you before about your language."

"Sorry, Aunt. It must be the virus." She and Tom exchanged their "Aren't grown-ups boring?" look. She lowered her voice. "Tomorrow I'll be dead, and then you'll be sorry." The door closed. Now Harry was bouncing up and down in bed with anticipation. "So what happened? Did you go?"

"Yes. Of course."

"And?"

So he told her, making it sound as scary and adventurous as he could. When he got to the bit about Nigel and the radio observatory Harry was not terribly pleased. "Bloody hell," she said. "You mean there were no guards?"

"Not exactly."

"And no torture chamber?"

59

"Er – no."

Harry was obviously thinking this through. Then she said: "That's okay." She sounded relieved. "There's still this big mystery about where your dad is?" That was Harry all over: she couldn't bear to be left out of the story.

"That's right." Tom couldn't keep it from her any longer. "And I've got another vital clue." Then he told her about Nigel's ideas and the newspaper's telephone number. He explained how his mother had turned the house into a concentration camp, and how his every move was watched. He said: "That's why I'm here. You've got to make contact with Nigel for me."

Harry thought about this for a moment. Then she said: "He doesn't sound very trustworthy to me. How do you know he's on our side?"

Tom was confused. "What do you mean?"

"These government people are very cunning. You ask my uncle. Perhaps this Nigel person is all part of the same plot. Perhaps he's under orders to get you as well."

Tom was shocked. "That's not possible. Nigel's just a nice bloke. He does in-depth interviews and local interest stories. You'd like him."

Harry looked serious. "Well, I'll phone him," she said, "but I'll have to be very suspicious. You can't be too careful," she added darkly.

So Tom gave her the phone number. "You will phone today, won't you?"

"I'm supposed to have flu," she replied. "My aunt will kill me if she sees me out of bed." Then she had an idea. "I know," she said, "you go down and keep her busy in the kitchen. Show her one of your boring card tricks or something. Then I can sneak through and use the phone in the bedroom."

Tom ignored the remark about his card tricks and went downstairs. Mrs Bell was plucking a chicken. Harry's aunt was round and jolly and liked to talk. He knew she was also fairly impressed with his puzzles. He decided that first of all he would make her feel good. You had to warm up your audience. He told her how much better Harry seemed. "You must be a very good nurse," he said slyly.

"Oh, I don't know. I expect she'll be up in day or two," said Mrs Bell, smiling. "But you're not to run off with her over that hill," she said waving the kitchen knife at him. Tom pretended not to understand.

Now it was time to distract her. He asked her if she would like to see his latest trick and produced a pack of cards. Of course she would. Tom cut the deck, swirled the pack into a fan the way they did in "The Cincinnatti Kid", and she chose a card. He thought hard: then he told her that her card was the Queen of Spades. He was right, of course. "Oh – that is clever!" she exclaimed. He was very pleased with her reaction, but of course he didn't show it. He shrugged. "It's just a trick," he said. "I know lots more difficult ones." He looked at the clock on the kitchen wall. He'd been down here for at least ten minutes. So he said quickly: "Oh I forgot. I left my satchel upstairs. I'll just go and get it. Then I'll be on my way home." *Before the Führer sends out the SS panzer divisions to arrest me.*

He raced upstairs. "Well?"

Harry was sitting up in bed looking very excited. "I've made contact," she said. "We've agreed to meet by the llama shed at two o'clock in two days time."

"We – you mean all three of us?"

"Well – if you want to come." Harry frowned at him. "He promised he'd keep it a secret, and so must you," she said fiercely.

"Are you still very suspicious?" asked Tom.

"Very," said Harry. "But he's our only hope, and that's all there is to it." They heard footsteps in the passage. "Quick. Beat it, before my aunt comes."

Tom wended his way homewards across the flatlands thinking about his mum and Harry's aunt. In *some* ways they could be quite nice and especially when they took you seriously and told you how clever you were. They were sort of, well, cosier than his dad or Harry's uncle. You might have a good time with your dad, but actually on a day-to-day basis you might prefer your mum (or Harry's aunt). And when you felt a bit unsure about things you'd be more likely to talk to your mum. He looked up at the sky. There was the evening star in the west. If you had to give it a personality, you'd probably say it was more like your mum than your dad. You could talk to a star like that quite easily and feel better. Which left only one big problem. *Why was Mrs Grant so horrible?* Perhaps locking her in the remote-controlled garage was the only cure after all.

Chapter Nine

NIGEL'S GOOD IDEA

The next two days went incredibly slowly. Tom passed the time trying to teach his baby sister to walk. He was very unsuccessful. *Of course* he said to himself, *she is only a girl*. Instead, he imagined she was a robot and attempted to programme instructions.

"You will walk one step," he said in his robot voice. The baby clutched the edge of the chair and made gurgling noises. "Your master speaks. You will walk one step."

It was no good. "She has no brain," he told his mother. "She needs a head transplant."

"Tom!" His mother was easily upset. "She can do a lot more than you could at that age."

"That's only because she has a first-class model," he replied smartly. It was strange, his dad not being here. It made him feel more grown-up in an odd sort of way.

He looked at his watch for the hundredth time that day. He realised that at last it was time to go.

He came up to his mother, who was doing the

ironing in front of the television, stood to attention and saluted. "Excuse me, Herr Fuhrer, may I have permission to go and see Harriet?"

Of course she did not get the joke. She said, putting down the iron with a sigh, "I'll telephone Mrs Bell." He watched her go through what he thought of as her concentration camp routine, and stood behind her, mimicking her words, "Yes, he's on his way now . . . You'll let me know if he's late . . . Yes, thank you . . . (a look at Tom) . . . he's behaving himself very well now . . . And how is poor Harriet?"

Jabber, jabber, jabber. He had to admit he felt confused about his feelings for his mum. He supposed it was because she loved him, all this Colditz stuff, but it was a bit hard to put up with at times. He wanted to say, "We're both in this together. You should trust me."

At last he was on his way across the fields to Harry's farm. The days of sun had ripened the waving seas of oats and barley to a golden yellow. He broke off an ear of corn and chewed it as he went. It was another wonderful day. The heat shimmered over the fields. Here and there white fenland poppies gleamed in the sunshine. The chalky smoke from the cement factory was ballooning up into a blue sky. Four orange cement mixers were driving slowly towards the main road. In the empty flatlands they looked like toys. He realised with a shock that he hadn't played with his own toys for a long time. Since his dad had disappeared in fact. That was another reason to be treated like a grown-up. It really was time he spoke to his mum about this.

When he arrived at the farm he found Harry and her mother in the kitchen. "Here I am, Mrs Bell, on schedule," said Tom, giving the Nazi salute. "I hope Harriet is better."

Harriet was sitting at the table chopping carrots. "Why, it's Mister Universe himself," she said sarcastically. She was obviously better. "Come and help me give this grub to Neddy," she said meaningfully.

They walked across the yard, carrying the llama's pail.

"Is he there yet?" Tom was full of anticipation.

"How do I know? I gave him directions. If he's too dumb to read a map, he won't be much good at finding your dad." It was clear from Harry's tone of voice that she had made a full recovery.

They went into the paddock and scattered Neddy's food into his pail. "You know, these animals are incredibly trendy," said Harry as they watched Neddy happily munching his vegetables. Tom never ceased to be amazed at the llama's capacity to spread joy and contentment in the most unlikely places.

Just as they were climbing the gate out of the llama paddock, Tom heard a familiar rattling sound. It was Apollo Thirteen with Nigel at the wheel.

"Here he is!" he exclaimed.

Nigel looked as much like a scarecrow as ever, except that today he was wearing dark glasses and this incredibly bright Hawaiian shirt. His blonde hair was straggling over his eyes and his pockets were bulging with notebooks, gadgets, spanners, old string etc. etc. He climbed out of the driving seat and jumped down.

"Hi there," said Nigel, shaking Tom's hand. "Is this your friend here? The one I spoke to on the phone?"

"Hello, I'm Harriet," she said, stepping forward

rather formally. Tom noticed that she was wearing new jeans.

He said: "Only everyone calls her Harry."

She paid no attention. "You thought I was joking about the llama, didn't you?" she said sharply. "Well, I wasn't." She pointed across to Neddy, placidly eating his lunch in the corner with his usual serene expression.

"It's a funny old world," said Nigel, admiring the llama from afar.

They watched Neddy in silence for a moment and then Tom could contain himself no longer. "So what's the news?" he said.

"What have you found out?" added Harry. Tom noticed that she seemed already less suspicious towards Nigel, but couldn't decide what this meant.

Nigel climbed up on the gate and began sucking a straw. "Where shall I begin?" he said out loud, as if thinking to himself.

"Begin at the beginning," said Harry. "And make sure you tell us everything."

"Sounds a good idea," said Nigel.

"Otherwise," she added menacingly, "we'll think you're on their side after all."

Nigel looked puzzled, an expression that Tom remembered from his first meeting. "On whose side?"

"The enemy's of course. The people in raincoats who took Tom's dad away and are torturing him –"

"Harry!" hissed Tom. "I told you that's not true!"

"That's only what you been *told*," she whispered back. "You've no proof."

Nigel sucked diplomatically on his straw. "Listen,

guys – how about I tell you my version, the story so far?"

"Okay," said Harry, "but we'll need good hard evidence."

So Nigel sat Tom and Harry on the ground and himself on the gate and began to talk in that calm and reasonable voice that Tom found so reassuring. For years afterwards Tom would remember this moment – the quiet of the summer afternoon, the sun high over the flatlands, and Nigel in his Hawaiian shirt brushing aside the hovering gnats as he talked.

He explained, to begin with, that the radio observatory over the hill was not alone. All over the countryside there were different kinds of tracking stations and observatories with telescopes looking up into the sky. "And what's more," he added, "they are all linked up."

"You mean like a telephone exchange," asked Tom, remembering what the Mekon had told him.

"Exactly," said Nigel. "And then there is radar. That's part of the system as well."

"Where does the radar fit in?" asked Harry.

Tom considered it was typical that Harry shouldn't know about radar. He was also a bit put out that she was suddenly showing an interest in all this simply because it was coming from a charming scarecrow in a Hawaiian shirt. She could have asked him about radar any time she liked and he'd have told her. *Typical. Absolutely typical.* Nigel's voice was purring in the background of his thoughts, answering Harry's interested questions.

"Telescopes watch the stars. Radar watches our world. Things like aeroplanes, helicopters, flocks of birds, thunderstorms. Radar stops things in the air crashing into each other."

"And radar watches for missiles, doesn't it?" said Tom, who had read about rockets and missiles. He wanted to show Harry that he knew about all this stuff as well.

"Yes, it also watches for missiles."

"Do your friends at the radio observatory watch for missiles?" asked Harry. There was, Tom thought, a note of admiration in her voice that was, as far as he was concerned, distinctly creepy. *It was typical. Absolutely typical.*

"Not really," said Nigel. "But some of the satellites they use are also able to tell them where the enemy keeps his missiles hidden."

Tom could see that Harry had been thinking. "But what's all this go to do with Tom's dad?"

"Oh. It's got a lot to do with him," said Nigel. "Tom's dad is a computer wizard. This system I've told you about is run by a family of computers. That's another network. And part of that network is run by his dad's office. Tom's dad is a very important bloke, you know."

"I know," said Tom proudly. (Actually, he didn't know exactly *how* important, but he didn't want Harry to realise that.)

"And," said Nigel, "like everything that's to do with computers and space and satellites and missiles and radar it's all very TOP SECRET."

"Of course," said Harry knowledgeably.

Tom was shocked by this showing off. *What do you know? You think computers are boring!*

"And so that means I've had to be very careful in

the way I've gone about asking questions," said Nigel.

He explained that a very good friend of his, "a contact", worked at the same office as Tom's dad. His friend had made a few discreet inquiries. Yes, Tom's dad was "away". The office had been told that he was on a "management course". Nigel had gone to the office with his friend and chatted to the woman on the desk. What had happened, apparently, was that one day, about three weeks ago, two men in raincoats had arrived at the reception area and asked to speak to Tom's dad. The next thing anyone knew was that Tom's dad was picking up his briefcase and following the two men out of the office to his car. The receptionist remembered it all so well. It was of course very official. The two men in raincoats had even signed their names in the visitors' book.

"What were their names?" asked Harry.

"Bodkin and Snowball," said Nigel, consulting his notebook.

"Perhaps they were the two men in raincoats I saw leaving our house when I came home from school," said Tom.

"What did they look like?" asked Nigel.

But all Tom could remember was the raincoats. "It was too far away and I couldn't really see." Then he had a brainwave. "But we can ask my mum," he said. "She talked to them."

"And I've had another good idea," said Nigel with a cunning smile. "There are lots of Bodkins in the local telephone directory. I've looked. But there's only one Snowball. I've got a funny feeling that we're going to have to pay him a little visit."

He jumped off the gate. "Come on," he said.

"That sounds like a very good idea," said Harry. "I'll just tell my aunt we're going to the village." It was obvious she wanted her share of the adventure too. What was more she was, Tom could tell, getting really stupid about Nigel.

—— Chapter Ten ——

CAPTAIN SNOWBALL

Apollo Thirteen bumped along the track to the main road. "First," said Nigel, "we have to find out what this Snowball character looks like." He looked at Tom with his scarecrow smile. "I think it's time you introduced me to your mum." He turned to Harriet. "Or am I still not to be trusted?"

"Don't be a dumb-bell," said Harry in her usual way. "Of course we trust you. That was just a test, that's all."

As they drove back to the village Tom began to wonder whether taking Nigel to see his mum was such a brainwave after all. He started to warn Nigel about his mother's current mood, explaining how strict she'd been with him lately. He heard her voice warning him about "strange men" and "trespassing". Yet here he was about to introduce her to an odd-looking journalist from the local newspaper with a special interest in the things that went on over the hill. It was, he considered, a suicide mission. But the more he thought about it, the more he realised he didn't have a choice. *I want my dad back. I've nothing to lose.*

Now Nigel was parking the land rover on the green outside the house. "Now the main thing," Tom was saying, "is not to upset her. So I'll just go in and see if she's about," he added, his heart sinking. Perhaps he could pretend she wasn't there.

But there was no chance of that. "We'll come with you," said Nigel cheerfully, jumping out of the driver's seat. He began lolloping across the grass, the tail of his Hawaiian shirt flapping behind him.

Tom and Harry ran to catch up. Tom rehearsed in his mind all the topics that he should try to avoid, at least to start with. The radio observatory. The newspaper. His dad's disappearance. The thing was for her to get to know Nigel as, well, as a sort of friend. Then, after a bit, they could work round to the vital subject of the investigation. "If you tell her you're interested in the radio observatory," he said breathlessly, catching up and tugging at Nigel's shirt, "she'll go bananas."

"Oh. Right-ho," said Nigel.

There was no way he could pretend she was out. They could hear the sound of a rolling pin in the kitchen, and sure enough there she was making a pie. "Hello, Mum," said Tom.

She looked up, rather startled.

When he saw the look of bewilderment on her face, he couldn't help himself. "This is Nigel, Mum," he blurted out. "He's a reporter. He's the bloke who gave me the lift. He's writing a story about the radio observatory over the hill. And he's going to help get Dad back."

He stopped. *Any minute now she's going to fly off her trolley.* There was the longest silence in the history of the world. Then, to Tom's amazement, his mother began to laugh. At first it was just a snigger, then half a chuckle, almost a laugh, and then she was giggling helplessly in the way that Tom hadn't seen for ages. He caught Nigel's eye, then Harry's, and suddenly they were all laughing in the most hilarious, rib-cracking kind of way you can imagine. Now his mum was kissing him and he could smell the pastry on her fingers. "You are a crazy one," she said.

Tom was so relieved he thought he was going to cry. And the more he thought about it afterwards he realised his mum was relieved, and grateful too.

Now it was Nigel's turn to tell his side of the story. Tom finally realised with a shock that his mum was really hopelessly in the dark about where his dad had got to. In fact, all she'd been told by the two men in raincoats was that he would be back "in due course", and that she was to "keep it to herself". And when Nigel asked her to describe the two men, all she could say was that the man called Snowball was at least six feet tall with gold-rimmed spectacles and a big beard.

Although it was a great relief she hadn't flown off her trolley after all, Tom felt (to be honest) a bit confused about what seemed like Nigel's winning ways. First, there was Harry behaving like a complete idiot to attract Nigel's attention. And now here was his mum chatting quite calmly about the men in raincoats (previously a big non-subject), as though it was the most natural thing in the world. Nigel seemed to have this effect on people. *Perhaps it's to do with that Hawaiian shirt. Or the dark glasses.* He made a mental note (as they talked) to get some dark glasses. Fast. Okay, Nigel was terrific, but why shouldn't Harry and his mum treat him with a bit of respect too?

After all, he thought to himself, *I'm the one who found Nigel in the first place. It's my dad, and it's my story.*

He came to with a start. His mother was shaking Nigel by the hand. "Thank you, Mr Williams," she was saying.

"Who the hell is Mr Williams?" Harry muttered to Tom.

Nigel was helpfully pointing his finger at himself, grinning from ear to ear like a lunatic. He was obviously very pleased with the way things had gone.

Now — *wow! amazement!* — his mother was saying it was fine to go off with Harry and Nigel in search of Snowball so long as he was back by six.

"No problem," said Tom. Feeling very grown-up, he began leading his friends out to the land rover.

"So," said Nigel, starting the engine, "shall we set off in search of the elusive Snowball?"

"Straight ahead, driver," said Tom, grandly. It was nice to be in charge again.

Nigel looked at Tom with his head on one side. "She's a nice lady, your mum," he said.

Tom nodded proudly. "You'll like my dad, too," he said, trying a bit of "positive thinking".

"Gosh," said Harry, as they swung onto the main road, tyres shrieking on the hot tarmac. "This is better than feeding the poxy llama."

Apollo Thirteen rattled across the flatlands towards the town. Nigel had a street map on his knee. "Here we are," he said. "Hollybush Drive. We want number Thirty-Three. But we've got to be careful. We don't want old Snowball to know what we are up to."

74

"Look." said Tom. "There it is."

You couldn't miss number Thirty-Three. The short driveway was guarded by a large black ornamental cannon. There was a tattered Union Jack flying from a tall white flagpole. The house itself was decorated with portholes, rigging and lifebuoys, and looked like an old-fashioned sailing ship.

"Cor," said Nigel. "Cor blimey!" He drove slowly past and they all looked in wonder. A few yards up the street he parked the land rover in the shade of a chestnut. "Now then," he said. "We've got to see if we've got the right house."

"How do we do that?"

Nigel thought for a minute. "Well, first of all I've got to find out if it's Snowball's. Then – " he paused. "Well, that's where you guys will come in. Wait right here for a moment. I'll just do my news-reporter bit. Won't be long." He winked at Harry. "Trust me."

Tom saw Harriet return the wink with a smile of pure devotion. *Harry in love! Give me a break!*

They watched him walking down the street with his gangly strides. "That shirt," said Harry, "is in the worst possible taste." Tom was not fooled. There was no mistaking the affection in her voice.

Nigel disappeared from view. They sat and waited. He seemed to be taking ages. Tom told Harry some interesting things about the solar system and the age of the universe. After a while she said, rather crossly, "You know all these things, but I bet you can't explain them."

Tom thought for a moment. "Why should I? Why should I always have to explain things?" he replied. Then to confuse her he added. "After all, the world is a banana."

She was puzzled. "What do you mean?"

He smiled. "What I say."

"But it doesn't make sense – 'the world is a banana.' What does it mean?"

He could see she didn't like it, as he'd hoped.

He remained annoyingly polite. "Lots of things don't make sense until you find the explanation. So the world is a banana."

"Don't keep saying that," she snapped.

A Mr Whippy van came jangling down the street, playing the theme tune from *The Godfather*. "I want an ice-cream," said Harry with irritation. "Where's your money?"

"Sorry. I left it at home." (Actually, he had a fifty pence piece in his pocket, but he didn't feel like sharing it with her just at the moment.)

"You're useless," said Harry, and went silent again. He knew she hated not to understand. Finally she said: "I can't stand this. Let's go and see what's going on."

As they started to walk slowly up the street they saw Nigel hurrying towards them, looking more than ever like a wind-up toy.

"Well," said Nigel, "*that* was an adventure."

Harry was full of questions: "Is it him? Is it the man in the raincoat?"

"It sure is," said Nigel. "Snowball is a retired navy Captain. A few years ago, he took up government security as as a second career. Funny bloke, though. He still wears his naval gear at weekends for old times sake."

Harry narrowed her eyes suspiciously. "He told you all this?"

"He knows I work on the newspaper and he'd even heard about my piece on the radio observatory. In fact he was surprisingly well-informed about me." Nigel shrugged. "I suppose it's not that odd. After all, Mondays to Fridays he's with the government security boys."

"Now what?" said Tom.

"Now it's your turn," said Nigel cheerfully. "I just quizzed him on his doorstep. It's up to you to case the joint."

"What for?" asked Tom nervously.

"For clues, moron," said Harry.

"We have to find out what he's done with your dad," said Nigel sympathetically.

"How?" asked Tom, feeling rather unsure. It was one thing to tackle your mum on a suicide mission, but this sounded a lot hairier.

"I don't know. Can't you pretend to be from the Scouts or something?"

"You are clever," said Harry, quite shameless in her admiration.

Tom knew he shouldn't feel jealous, but there it was, he did. *Why doesn't she ever say nice things about me?* Out loud he said: "Well, we can try," rather resolutely. If this was the only way to get Harry's attention, there was nothing for it.

"That's the spirit," said Nigel. "Don't worry. I'll be on the look-out."

So Tom and Harry set off towards number Thirty-Three while Nigel watched from the front of the land rover. Outside number Thirty-Three they paused. It seemed very still and quiet. Tom felt distinctly nervous.

"I wonder what's happening inside," he said, trying not to think of the torturers.

"Come on," said Harry, walking towards the front door. "Nigel's right. We'll pretend we're from the Scouts. We'll tell Snowball it's his turn for a Good Deed."

There was a rusty anchor by the side of the front door. As they pressed the bell they heard a booming laugh from within, heavy footsteps, and then the sound of a chain rattling as the door was unlocked.

"I'm scared," said Tom, "let's run."

"Don't be a creep," said Harry. She was obviously terrified as well. "If you bunk off now I'll never speak – "

She broke off in mid-sentence. The door opened. There, in a navy blue uniform with smart gold buttons was a tall, imposing elderly man with an immense sailor's beard and gold glasses. "Ahoy there, kids," said a booming voice high above them. "What can I do you for?"

"We're from the Scouts," said Tom in a very small squeak.

"And we've come to do a Good Deed," said Harry.

"Nice of you to offer, boys," boomed Captain Snowball. "Let me see . . . as a matter of fact . . . yes, I think you can help me. Come in, come in. Let me introduce myself. Captain Snowball, Royal Navy, Retired."

Harry and Tom hesitated on the doormat.

"Step aboard, step aboard," said Captain Snowball, ushering them into the gloomy hallway.

Inside, the house was as strange as outside, and as gloomy as a coffin. There was also this incredible ticking sound. Tick-tick-tick. Tick-tock. Tick-tock. Tockety-tockety-tock. Tom realised that the place was full of clocks. He and Harry looked about them in amazement.

"I can see," said Captain Snowball, speaking very slowly, as if giving dictation to an invisible secretary, "that you are intrigued by these clocks. It's my own collection. All set for different times." He began to give a guided tour, pointing as he went. "Now in this corner we have the mysterious East – Japan, Hong Kong, Shanghai, Bangkok, Singapore and Manila . . ." He lumbered towards a cluster of grandfather clocks. "Here we have the Mediterranean – Athens, Rome, Marseilles, Cairo." He shook his head. "Madrid. I fear, is not working at the moment, and Rome is losing half an hour a day." He looked keenly at Tom. "I expect you know about Time," he said.

"Yes," said Tom, remembering Nigel's words. "Everything is relative."

"That's it! That's it!" He patted Harry on the head. Harry scowled. "Is this your brother?"

"Yes," said Tom quickly, digging Harry in the ribs. He smiled to himself, and began to feel more relaxed. Old Snowball obviously had nothing to do with any torturing.

Now that Nigel wasn't around, Tom was eager to show off a bit in front of Harry. He started in on some obvious questions like Was he the captain of a British warship? and Did he fight in the Falklands?

"Alas," said Captain Snowball, "I was very much of the modern navy. I hardly ever went to sea. Before my retirement, I spent the last ten years marooned in dry-dock at a desk in the civil service." He seemed to find this funny for no reason that Tom could see, and he laughed in a way that Tom found rather sinister. Thinking about in later, there was something disturbing about Captain Snowball's good humour, something he did not trust.

"Now then, kids," boomed Captain Snowball. "That's enough chin-wagging. It's time to get down to brass tacks. I've got a nice little job for you right here."

And so saying he led the way up the creaky staircase to the first floor.

"Perhaps he's got your dad hidden here somewhere," whispered Harry.

"Ssssshhh!" said Tom.

"Now then, lads," said Captain Snowball, "you would do me a big favour if you could help polish the brass on these clocks."

There were even more clocks upstairs – tall clocks, short clocks, eight-day-clocks, calendar clocks, alarm clocks, electric and digital clocks. In Snowball's bedroom there were hourglasses, barometers, metronomes, even a barograph with purple ink. The rooms were very dark with a lot of heavy Victorian furniture.

Snowball handed out dusters and polish and they started work. Snowball stood and watched, telling them things that Tom at least found quite interesting about his collection.

They'd been polishing away for quite a while and getting warm with the work when the phone rang.

"Excuse me, lads," said Captain Snowball.

They heard him lumbering downstairs.

"Quick," said Harry. "Now's our chance."

They began racing through each room, looking for

clues. As they searched they could hear Captain Snowball chatting away downstairs.

Higher and higher they went, right up to the attic floor. They were almost in the last room in the house and Tom was about to give up hope when Harry said, in a stage whisper, "Look!"

"What?" Tom whispered back.

"Do you see what I see?"

She was pointing at the wall. There was a black-and-white photograph, surrounded by nautical charts and Vicorian prints. They went closer. It was an aerial view of the flatlands. "Look," said Harry, "it's our village. There's the cement factory. There's the radio observatory and there's – " She stopped. "Look at that," she whispered with excitement. Dotted across the photograph were a number of little white flags. And right on the site of Tom's house there was a little white flag with a date written in neat black ink.

"Wow!" said Tom, peering closer. "That's the day my dad disappeared."

The Captain was calling from downstairs. "We'll have to go," said Harry. They came downstairs trying to act as naturally as possible. "And what have you two rascals been up to?" boomed Captain Snowball.

"Just admiring your collection," said Tom.

"We've finished polishing," said Harry, which was a bit of a lie.

"Well done, lads," said Captain Snowball. "A good deed is a good deed." And he gave them each a pound.

They said thank you and goodbye and walked back down the street to Nigel's land rover.

"Should we tell Nigel about the money?" asked Tom.

"Don't be stupid," said Harry, "Of course not."

Nigel was thrilled to hear about the aerial photo. "I knew you'd find an important clue," he said. "Well done, team."

"It was lucky the phone went." said Tom.

Nigel looked rather pleased with himself. "That was easy. I got the office to call him."

"You are clever," said Harry again.

This fan club stuff was getting dangerously out of hand in Tom's opinion. He said: "So now the question is – how does Snowball fit into the puzzle?"

"There's only one way to find out," said Nigel.

"What's that?" Tom fingered the pound in his pocket uneasily.

"Listen in to his conversation."

"How will we do that?"

Nigel had a mysterious smile. "I think it's time I introduced you to my old friend Suzanne," he said. "Then you'll see how."

"I wonder who Suzanne is," said Tom, after Nigel had dropped them back at the village.

Harry was looking sulky. "Probably some stinky old girl-friend," she said crossly. "Though I can't see what she's got to do with listening in on Captain Snowball."

Chapter Eleven

ENTER MR BODKIN

They didn't have to wait long to find out about Suzanne. On Monday after school Tom and Harry were in the tree-house talking over the meaning of the aerial photo when a battered white Transit van pulled up on the green outside. Then a man in a brown lab. coat jumped out. It was Nigel.

They scrambled down the rope-ladder and ran out to the van.

"Hi, kids," said Nigel. "This is my old lady," he went on, patting the van fondly. "Suzanne. The best secret listening machine in the world." They followed him round to the back. Nigel creaked open the doors. Inside was all kinds of complicated-looking equipment, coloured wires, screens, spools and headphones.

"I bet you stole half that stuff," said Harry in her usual blunt way. Tom could see that her eyes were shining with happiness and admiration. *What a disgusting exhibition!*

"All of it!" said Nigel cheerfully. "I'm the Most Wanted Man in the district. Jump in, guys," he said, closing the doors. "Now," he went on, as they set off towards the town, "let's see what Captain Snowball is talking about on that telephone of his."

Like Apollo Thirteen, Suzanne was not the fastest machine on the road, but soon they were cruising into Hollybush Drive. They parked some way from number Thirty-Three, and then they all climbed into the back and closed the doors behind them. From the outside, Suzanne looked completely harmless, an old crock parked in a quiet back street. Inside, Nigel began to switch things on and fiddle with her knobs. Strange squeaks and whistles came out of the equipment. Then they heard an unmistakable sound.

"Tick-tock. Tock-tock. Tockety-tock."

Tom tugged Nigel's sleeve in excitement. "Snowball's clocks," he whispered. Nigel twiddled the knobs some more, but all they could hear was the weird ticking. "He must be out. We'll have to wait."

So they waited. And waited. And waited.

It was very stuffy in the back of the van, and Nigel instructed them to keep very quiet. There wasn't much light, either. If they hadn't been so keen to hear Snowball, it would have been very boring. Nigel sat hunched over his equipment in his headphones. Tom and Harry played noughts and crosses; scissors, paper, stone; and hangman. Suddenly, Nigel said, "Sssshhh!!" They all held their breath. Nigel fiddled with the knobs. The sound of heavy footsteps came over the radio. Then they heard a grunt.

Nigel switched on his tape-recorder. The spools began to turn. Swish-click-swish-click-swish-click.

84

Then they heard Captain Snowball's voice booming out. "Snowball to Control. Incoming. Roger."

"Roger. Control to Snowball. Affirmative. Over."

"I don't recognise that voice," whispered Nigel.

Snowball was talking again. "How is pre-test count-down? Over."

"Pre-test countdown is A-OK. Over."

Then another voice said: "Do we have full laser-bay integrity? Over." Tom was confused. He couldn't follow any of this.

"Affirmative. Laser-bay is dynamic. Over."

There was a burst of static. "They're talking about something to do with advanced laser technology," said Nigel. "It sounds like some kind of test."

"I bet that's what my dad is involved with," said Tom.

"I'm sure of it," whispered Nigel.

"But what does it all mean?" asked Tom. It was that feeling he sometimes had with the stars. He was baffled, bewildered, frightened.

"I don't know," Nigel was very tense. "We'll have to analyse it later."

"Where is he?" asked Tom. His dad was so close it seemed, and yet there was this wall of double-dutch in the way. He felt incredibly frustrated.

"That's what we've got to find out." Nigel was bending over his machinery. "I have to locate the radio source for this Control person," he said. "At the moment all we can do is listen."

They could hear Captain Snowball having a conversation with what sounded like another security guard. "Will he talk to the torturers?" asked Harry.

Tom was about to say *Don't be silly, Harry, you know there aren't any torturers*, when Nigel sat up with a start.

85

"Uh-oh," he said.

"What's the matter?"

"Listen."

The voice on the radio was speaking very urgently. "Control to Snowball. Control to Snowball. Criticality One Situation. You have interference. Repeat you have interference."

Nigel pulled off the headphones and began flicking off the switches in front of him. He pulled the tape spool off the sprocket. "Here," he said to Tom, "stick that in a safe place. It might come in handy." Tom took the tape-recording and put it in his school satchel. "Time we were moving on, I think," said Nigel, trying not to sound hurried.

He clambered through into the driving seat. The engine coughed once, twice and then groaned. "Come on, Suzanne," said Nigel. He tried again.

The engine spluttered and died.

Nigel jumped out. "There's no time to lose," he shouted. "They'll be here any minute. We'll have to push-start the old lady." He began to give directions. Harry, who worked on her uncle's farm, knew about tractors and gears. She climbed into the driving seat. Nigel and Tom started to push Suzanne down the street.

"Push!" shrieked Harry.

"We're pushing," they shouted. Suzanne seemed stuck.

"Of course!" exclaimed Nigel, "we've left the brake on!" He rushed to the front and released the hand-brake.

"Now!" he cried. "All together!" They began to push again. But Suzanne was loaded down with all

Nigel's gear. The road was flat. The van hardly moved at all.

As they stood on the kerb rather out of breath, wondering what to do next, Tom noticed two half-familiar figures in raincoats strolling casually down the pavement.

"Good afternoon," said Captain Snowball. "You seen a bit becalmed. Having a spot of engine trouble?"

"Oh, hello," said Nigel evasively.

"Mr Williams," said Captain Snowball courteously, "I don't think you know my colleague, Mr Bodkin."

"Pleased to meet you, Mr Williams," said the other man, with a smile like a razor blade.

— Chapter Twelve —

THE BLACK BMW

In his office clothes, Captain Snowball looked quite different from the weekend. Now his beard seemed fierce not jolly, the eyes behind the gold-rimmed glasses seemed cold not welcoming, and his vast bulk in its familiar raincoat seemed threatening not reassuring.

Mr Bodkin was even worse. He was so colourless he looked, thought Tom, as if he were dead. His eyes were grey, his skin was grey, the hair plastered on his head was grey, and of course even his raincoat was grey, government issue. The only colour about him was the little red notebook he held in his grey right hand.

Now it was Mr Bodkin's turn to speak. "Surely, Mr Williams, you should be reporting for duty in the newsroom this afternoon, not fooling around with a couple of school-children?"

"I – I – we have been conducting some experiments – I mean – " Tom could see that Nigel was obviously very nervous. "It's – it's – I'm teaching them about science, you know."

"Perhaps," said Mr Bodkin in his cold grey voice, "you would care to show my colleague and I exactly what, in the scientific line, you have in your van. It is *your* van, I take it," he added nastily.

"If it hadn't been mine, it would have started quicker and we wouldn't be here," muttered Nigel under his breath as he opened the double doors at the back.

Mr Bodkin and Captain Snowball crowded round.

"Very interesting, Mr Williams," observed Mr Bodkin. "You have some, er, typically ingenious listening devices here." Now he opened his cherry red notebook. "Eavesdropping is not a pretty word, Mr Williams. Would you care to tell us whose conversations you found so fascinating?"

Nigel said nothing. Harriet ran her finger through the dust on the winderscreen. Tom hugged the satchel with the tape-recording closer to him and stared defiantly at the two officials.

"May I suggest," Mr Bodkin went on, in his monotonous grey voice, "that you were attempting to eavesdrop" – he made the word sound especially criminal – "on the private conversations of my colleague here, Captain Snowball?"

As Nigel began stammering again, more than ever like a scarecrow, Tom found himself becoming suddenly courageous. "No, we weren't," he said boldly. "We were listening to your laser test countdown." There was a stunned silence. Mr Bodkin and Captain Snowball looked at each other meaningfully. Then Mr Bodkin attempted a let's-not-get-too-serious kind of smile and said, "I'm sorry, sonny, I don't quite follow you."

"Oh yes, you do," said Tom, feeling more and more confident. "You know very well it's all to do with my dad, and it's incredibly secret, of course." He paused for effect. "The trouble is we know all about it."

Nigel suddenly perked up. "That's right. We know all about it."

Now it was Mr Bodkin's turn to start stammering. "Wha – wha – what do you mean?"

"Not only do we know all about it," added Nigel, pointing at Tom's satchel, "we also have it on magnetic tape."

Mr Bodkin stepped towards Tom with his hand out. "Now then, sonny – " he began. Tom backed away towards Harry.

But Nigel was interrupting. "I can assure you, Mr Bodkin, that there are quite a few newspaper editors, friends of mine, who would be very interested to see the transcript of that tape."

"You'll never get away with this," muttered Mr Bodkin.

"Oh, yes we will," said Tom. "You can't make me hand this over." Then a thought occurred to him. "Unless, of course, you can help us with a little problem we've got concerning a certain missing person."

"You – you – you mean – " flustered Mr Bodkin.

"That's right," said Tom, folding his arms defiantly round the satchel. "My dad."

Mr Bodkin looked at Captain Snowball, frowning in thought. Then he pulled a tiny two-way radio out of his raincoat pocket and began speaking in a strange kind of gobbledygook to someone at the other end.

Before any of them could say Crab Nebula two police cars with flashing lights were racing towards them down Hollybush Drive and had pulled up with wailing sirens next to Suzanne.

Now that things were going his way, Tom tried to feel calmer, but his insides were like jelly. "The main thing," he said to Harry under his breath, "is that we stick together." She nodded. He found himself putting his hand in hers, and amazingly enough she gave it a big, encouraging squeeze. He felt a lot better.

They stood on the kerb and watched the policemen fussing round Suzanne. Mr Bodkin was giving orders for her to be towed away for repairs.

"Look," said Harry. Tom turned. Cruising slowly towards them was a black BMW. Harry tugged at his sleeve. "Look!" she whispered. "The number!"

And there it was again: CYW D 505.

The chauffeur got out and opened all the doors. Mr Bodkin turned to Nigel: "Mr Williams, if you and these children would like to come with me I may perhaps have something of interest to show you."

Children! Tom put on his toughest expression. He wanted to say something to this horrible grey creep in the raincoat like "I'm ten years old and don't you forget it", but he kept his mouth shut. It was clear they'd got Mr Bodkin on the run. *What's this "may perhaps"!? Who are you kidding?* thought Tom, glaring at Bodkin and Snowball.

"Where are we going?" he muttered to Nigel as they crowded together into the back seat with Mr Bodkin, the satchel with the tape-recording safely round his shoulder. (Captain Snowball took the front seat next to the chauffeur with Harry sitting stiffly on his knee.)

91

Nigel said nothing, but Captain Snowball, who had overheard, said "If I was you, sonny, I wouldn't ask too may questions till we get there."

Soon the black BMW was racing across the flatlands. Tom recognised the direction they were going in. Away in the distance in front of them he could see the chalky white smoke from the cement factory. *Perhaps we're going to the radio observatory*. But no, they drove past the seven white satellite saucers and turned up the hill towards Tom's village. Perhaps they were being taken straight home, he thought. *Mum will get a surprise.*

But it wasn't his mum who got the surprise, it was Tom. As the black BMW came down the long hill towards the village, it began to slow down. *I don't believe it*, said Tom to himself. *We can't be!*

But they were. The car swung to the right and pulled up at the checkpoint. They were going into the cement factory.

Chapter Thirteen

THE CEMENT FACTORY

It was weird to be going inside the monster of his imagination, but here was the security man at the gate nodding them through. The chauffeur drove past four orange cement trucks parked in front of a huge cement chute that reminded Tom of the slide in the school swimming pool. The factory towered over them: chimneys, chalk mills, mountains of grey cement. They could hear the grinding of the machinery even through the bullet-proof glass of the black BMW. Strangest of all, there was no one in sight. The car crunched down a track running between the works, and was waved through a second check-point. Ahead, Tom could see the tall, white cliffs of the quarry behind the factory. *Where on earth are we going?* he wondered. The track seemed to run straight into –

"Wow!" said Tom.

In front of them as they turned the corner, stretching into the hillside itself, was a long tunnel. All at once they were driving on smooth tarmac, like a motorway underpass, beneath the hill. It, too, was completely deserted. Tom began to count the lights on the wall as they flashed past, one, two, three . . . twenty-five, twenty-six . . . They were slowing down. They must be at least a mile under the hill. He remembered Harry's words: "*He's probably under-ground in a special concrete dungeon.*"

He leant forward and whispered: "Well done, Harry." But she was too preoccupied with what was happening to hear him. Now the car had stopped and Mr Bodkin was getting out. He seemed more at home in this grey underworld. "Here we are," he said, as if it was the jolliest place imaginable.

Tom, Harry and Nigel got out, stretching awkwardly after their ride. It was very cold and still. Tom thought he could hear the sound of water dripping, and somewhere further underground there was a cavernous booming, like a door slamming.

In front of them was a steel grille. Above it a red Exit sign flashed on and off. Mr Bodkin took a sort of credit card out of his wallet. He inserted this into the computerised lock, punched in a set of numbers and the grille slid aside with a menacing hum. In front of them was an armed guard behind a desk, watching football on a small portable TV. He stood up when he saw Mr Bodkin, who flashed his ID card and hurried them through. Tom thought: *So she was right about the guards as well.* But this time he didn't say anything.

They followed Mr Bodkin down a long, brightly lit corridor. It was like walking down the inside of a fluorescent light tube. Tom and the others squinted in the glare. Behind them, lumbering along on his own, humming a little tune, Captain Snowball brought up the rear. They met no one. Occasionally, at a turn in the passage, there would be a closed-circuit television with a red eye. From time to time, the Tannoy system would crackle into life: "Brian Simmons – com. line check-in, please", or "Alan McAlpine – main-frame read-out, please."

They were standing outside a door marked 101. Mr Bodkin hesitated for a moment as if all this was the worst idea in the world, but then his eye fell on Tom's satchel and he took out his credit card again. The door slid open as before and they all crowded curiously into a small antechamber. Inside, there was another door marked TOP SECRET. "Is this your torture chamber?" asked Harry, trying to crack a joke.

Mr Bodkin faced her with a humourless stare. "My dear girl, this is a civilised country. We don't use torture."

Harry looked very disappointed.

Now Mr Bodkin began marshalling his visitors. There was a little booth like the ones Tom had seen on railway stations for passport photos. "Stand still," he commanded, lining them up.

There was a flash, and the machine produced a polaroid print of Nigel looking even more like a scarecrow. Then it was Harry's turn. Then Tom's. He noticed that they were all too anxious to compare their likenesses. Harry's teeth were chattering with cold. Now Captain Snowball was making up plastic security badges for them. "Wear these at all times," he said, "or you'll get into serious trouble."

Mr Bodkin went over to a keyboard in the wall by the door marked TOP SECRET. He typed in a codeword, and a lot of paper came spewing out. He separated the pages and began handing them round. "You have to sign this," he said coldly, "before you go any further."

Mr Bodkin looked incredibly grave. Tom could see that he did not like visitors, even when he had no choice.

"What is this?" asked Harriet.

"It's the Official Secrets Act of course." Mr Bodkin was full of contempt. "Don't they teach you anything at school these days? Once you've signed it, you have to keep everything you see here to yourselves." He gave them his grey, headmasterly stare.

They all nodded and passed the biro round. When Tom signed he kept his fingers crossed, so it wouldn't count. *I bet Harry's done the same.* It would be good to talk this over later, assuming that there was going to be a "later".

He came out of his thoughts. Captain Snowball was tapping him on the shoulder. "Cheer up, sonny. Don't mind about old Bodders. His bark is worse than his bite."

Mr Bodkin collected up all the documents, handed them with a curt nod to Captain Snowball and pressed another button in the wall. The door opened and they walked into what looked like the largest electronic workshop in the world, the size of an aircraft hangar, hollowed out of the hill. It was, Tom said afterwards, like going into the fourth dimension, into another world. For a moment no one said anything as they all looked about in stunned amazement.

— Chapter Fourteen —

THE INSIDE STORY

Everywhere they turned there were coloured wires, power units, flashing lights, flickering screens, piles of technical journals, and yellow and blue racks of computer tape. Here and there, to remind the technicians of the world above them outside, there were enormous indoor plants – busy lizzies, rubber plants, ferns and creepers.

Tom had always imagined that scientists worked in a kind of electronic silence, disturbed only by the hum and whirr of disc-drives and the crackle of static electricity. But this place was pandemonium, what his dad would call "Bedlam". It was a bit like the garage where they had the car serviced – only a hundred, a thousand times, bigger.

As well as the interruptions from the paging system, there were different kinds of music from all corners of the workshop, all blaring out together. "Dreamer, you always were a dreamer . . ." floated up from one workbench. Nearby, another group of slightly older technicians were playing hit singles from the Sixties as they worked. Tom noticed that Nigel had cheered up a lot and was now actually humming along with the music: ". . . in the house of the rising sun . . ."

It seemed to Tom an odd place for Mr Bodkin to be involved with. He and Captain Snowball were so stiff and formal. All the boffins here wore blue jeans and running shoes. They seemed to live on junk food, Big Macs, Whoppers and Yorkies, and wherever you looked there were piles of empty Coca-cola cans. Tom could see that none of the engineers were much older than Nigel, and some of them looked rather like him in his troll/scarecrow mode. In fact, they looked like students from the university in the nearby town.

The little group of visitors followed Mr Bodkin along a metal walkway suspended above the chaotic bustle of the workshop and into a smaller office marked XRASER COMMAND.

"This," said Mr Bodkin in a low, awesome voice, "is the Holy of Holies, the Defence of the Realm."

The Defence of the Realm office was also in chaos, piled high with computer print-out paper, magazines, old Coke cans, floppy discs and magnetic tape. On the wall there was an enormous TV screen. Mr Bodkin went over to the desk, moved a half-eaten pizza off the control panel and pressed a switch.

The familiar outline of the country flashed up in laser-thin red tracing on the screen. "Look." He pressed another switch. "There is our navy. And there – " click " – the American nuclear submarine fleet." Another click. "These are all the aeroplanes flying overhead at this minute, and here – " click " – all our missiles in their bunkers." The screen changed again. "And here," he concluded, "are all our missile warning stations."

"That's where your dad works," said Nigel, pointing helpfully.

Tom had been thinking about his father all the time during the visit but had decided not to say anything unless Mr Bodkin didn't keep his part of the bargain. But now that Nigel had brought the subject up, he felt encouraged to say, "Yes, where is my dad, Mr Bodkin?"

Mr Bodkin's grey lips remained as thin as razorblades, and his eyes as hard as meteorites. "I am coming to that," he said without emotion. He threw another switch and the screen in front of them went off.

Tom decided to press on. "It was you that I saw leaving our house, wasn't it?"

"It must be," added Harry recklessly, "because we found your aerial reconnaissance photographs in Captain Snowball's house."

Mr Bodkin's face was as blank as the TV screen. "I have no idea what you are talking about," he said, and Tom felt afraid to say more. It was one thing to get inside a Top Secret organisation, but it might be quite another to get out again.

Just at this moment, a siren began wailing outside the Defence of the Realm office. They all turned round, but Captain Snowball reassured them that it was only what he called "a pre-test warning siren". *Whatever that means.* "Eight bells, eight bells. All hands on deck." And so saying, he walked out of the office towards a sign marked RED ZONE 7. *Wonder where he's off to*, thought Tom.

Before Tom had a chance to find out where Captain Snowball had gone, Nigel said: "Look, I do think you should explain where this lad's father has got to." He sounded very reasonable and Tom thought: *Good old Nigel*.

"I am coming to that, Mr Williams," repeated Mr Bodkin crossly. "First we have an important experiment to observe." Click. Now the TV screen showed a section of the workshop floor not visible from where they were. Tom could see dozens of technicians working on a massive white steel grid criss-crossed with dozens of strange blue tubes. They looked like children on a vast climbing frame. Naturally he wanted to know what it was.

"This is our X-ray laser, of course," said Mr Bodkin. "We are about to run a very significant test."

As if to echo his words, the Tannoy came to life. "Attention in the laser bay," said an American voice. "In two minutes power conditioning will begin an automatic charging sequence. At this time, all personnel will clear the laser bay."

Nigel bent close to Tom's ear. "That's because of the voltage in the capacitors. The power surge could kill someone if there was an accident."

A buzzer sounded. "Attention in the laser bay. Tower conditioning will initiate an automatic charging sequence. Three . . . two . . . one . . ."

Nigel leant forward again, pointing helpfully. "Look, now the computer's in control."

They could see on the TV monitor the laser area cleared of technicians. The giant white climbing frame with its blue tubes was bathed in an eerie grey light.

"Sequence started," said a synthesised voice from

the control panel. On another TV monitor a yellow arrow moved jerkily down a long checklist of computer tasks.

"The laser will fire in one hundred and twenty seconds," said the synthesised voice.

They watched in silence. Tom peeped down on to the workshop floor. Now all the technicians were silent too, and still.

The computer began the final countdown: "Five . . . four . . . three . . . two . . . one . . ."

There was a barely audible distant SNAP! But on the TV monitor Tom could see a vast transformation of energy as ten billion watts of power surged into flash lamps and laser amplifiers.

There was a pause. The tension on the workshop floor was over. A buzz of conversation started. "One day," said Mr Bodkin, a strange gleam in his eye, "that will be the ultimate defence of the realm." He thought about what he had said for a moment. "The ultimate."

"What's it got to do with my dad?" asked Tom.

"You saw the computer running the test," said Mr Bodkin. "That's part of your father's responsibility."

"Why isn't he here, then?"

"Because – because he is analysing its performance in relation to the main-frame." His voice became even chillier. "He is also evaluating the interstellar capabilities of the system."

Tom realised he'd only got the faintest clue what Mr Bodkin was talking about, but he said, "Of course," anyway. It wouldn't do to let Mr Bodkin think he was getting on top again. *One day I'll get my dad to explain everything.*

"Now if you look carefully," Mr Bodkin was saying, "you can see that our boys are working on the design and construction of a new generation of high-speed computers to target the X-ray laser."

There was another click and the camera zoomed in close-up to one of the work benches. It was scattered with transistors, wire, light bulbs and soldering iron, and reminded Tom of his dad's workbench at home.

"This is the kind of work," explained Mr Bodkin, "that keeps us ahead of the Other Side."

"The Other Side? What Other Side?" asked Harry.

"We all know who the Other Side is," said Mr Bodkin firmly.

Nigel brightened up and pulled out his reporter's notebook.

Mr Bodkin reached out and lifted Nigel's biro from his grasp. "Mr Williams, please! We are talking of the Defence of the Realm."

"Excuse me," said Nigel, looking a bit like a crumpled balloon.

"Is the Defence of the Realm what my dad does all day?" asked Tom.

"I'm coming to that. Really, you are very inquisitive young man."

"Look," said Tom, as politely as possible, "I just want my dad back. That's all."

Mr Bodkin did not seem very interested in that side of things. He began to explain that the most important computers were the ones that invented codes for the X-ray laser. "The trouble is that if the Other Side knows all about your computers they know about the Defence of the Realm."

"Well, that's obvious," said Harry. *Showing off in front of Nigel again.*

Mr Bodkin seemed a bit taken aback. "So that's why we have to have very clever people inventing cleverer and cleverer computers to be one jump ahead of the Other Side."

"That's what Tom's dad does, I suppose," said Harry, butting in again. "So why has he disappeared?" The thing about Harry, Tom realised when he thought about it afterwards, was that she was as tactful as a rhinoceros.

Mr Bodkin raised a thin grey eyebrow. "Disappeared?" Click. The picture on the screen changed again. The hidden camera was roving from face to face, and Nigel was making funny Nigel-type noises as he recognised people he was writing about for the newspaper. Then it stopped and focused on a scientist peering at a silicon-chip circuit.

Tom thought he was going to faint. *Yes, yes! It's my dad!* Right there, working on a new invention for X-ray lasers. He was just as he remembered him, totally absorbed in his work. But his first thought was: *It must be a film.* He panicked and said:

"It's not real. It can't be. It's a video. Harry was right after all. You've tortured him to death."

Mr Bodkin never lost his composure. "You are a very excitable young man – "

Tom thought: *You pompous old fool.*

Nigel was putting a hand on his shoulder and speaking in that calm way of his. "It's okay, mate. It's not a recording. It's for real. Your dad's fine. Look," he said, pointing at the digital clock on the wall. "The time's the same as the one on the monitor."

Now there were tears of joy in Tom's eyes, but he blew his nose to hide his emotion. *I can't have Harry see me behaving like a wet.* And he didn't want Nigel to forget that he was at least ten years old and not a child any more.

Mr Bodkin was saying that of course it was not a video, and that of course his dad was somewhere not far away in the X-ray laser bay. And then of course Harry was wanting to know what had happened to him. Tom listened in a daze, watching his dad all the while on the monitor.

Then the screen went blank and they were being invited to sit in the swivel chairs by the control desk. Tom noticed that Captain Snowball still had not returned and wondered vaguely what he was up to. *Anything is possible here.* He also noticed that Harry was sitting next to Nigel with that ridiculous expression of admiration in her eyes which didn't, in his view, suit her at all.

He came to with a start. *Panic! Panic!* What had he missed? Mr Bodkin was droning on in his weather-forecaster's voice of his: " . . . computer analysis showed that the secrets of the X-ray laser technology were being reproduced by the Other Side. Naturally, our masters in government were anxious to establish the reason for this." He paused and considered Tom carefully for a moment. "Now I regret to say that your father had to be exposed to what we call "positive vetting" for a number of weeks before we –"

"So he *was* tortured!" Harrry exclaimed. "I knew I was right." She leant across Mr Bodkin with an expression almost of approval. "Do you use electric toasters or do you put hoods over their heads and beat them with sticks?"

Mr Bodkin looked as though he was going to be sick. He looked at Harry with distaste. "Positive vetting is not torture," he said stiffly. "We had to be certain that our suspicions were groundless." He returned to Tom. "It's now clear that your father was the victim of a vicious plot."

"A plot?" said Nigel. "Good-oh," he said. "I like a bit of suspense."

Mr Bodkin obviously thought this remark in poor taste as well. Ignoring Harry and Nigel, he continued his explanation to Tom. "Your father is a very clever man. We now know that the Other Side was, er, following his work on the computerised co-ordination of the X-ray laser we have just seen in action. They were afraid that the X-ray laser was going to make the Defence of the Realm invincible." He paused dramatically. "So what did they do?"

"I haven't the faintest," said Tom, who was still trying to work out what "computerised co-ordination of the X-ray laser" meant.

"They tried to discredit him," said Mr Bodkin. "They tried to make us think that he was on their side."

"You mean he was framed," Nigel interrupted.

"If you wish to put it in that lurid way, Mr Williams," said Mr Bodkin coldly.

"I can't help it," said Nigel. "I'm just doing my job."

Tom had got one thing straight, though. He now understood why his dad had been so reluctant to talk about the radio observatory just before he disappeared. He must have been very worried by all this "framing" by the Other Side. Tom made a mental note to ask Nigel exactly what "framing" meant. He caught Mr Bodkin's eye. "Can I go and say hello to him?"

Mr Bodkin looked doubtful. "You have to understand, young man, this is a Top Secret installation. Personnel movement here is highly restricted." He appeared to be thinking aloud. "On the other hand the testing of the X-ray laser has now been successfully completed. Perhaps . . . I don't see why you shouldn't, er, greet him on the video link."

Mr Bodkin picked up the remote control and switched on the TV screen in the office. There was Tom's dad in front of them again, discussing something with a very young-looking scientist. Mr Bodkin murmured something into his two-way radio. The Tannoy sprang to life and the same American voice started talking in a strange language Tom couldn't follow. But it obviously meant something to his dad. They watched him walk over to a closed circuit TV screen and now he was looking directly at them.

Tom waved. "Hello, Dad. It's me, Tom," he shouted, even though there was no sound.

For a moment, his father looked as though he had seen a ghost. Then he waved back. There was still no sound, but you could see he was saying "Hello, Tom." He seemed very excited.

"That's enough," said Mr Bodkin, who looked to Tom like someone who had never had a real dad. The screen went blank. "Your father will be returning to normal duties very soon."

"You mean I can have my dad back?"

"If you want to put it that way," said Mr Bodkin in his government security-officer voice.

"How soon is soon? Will he be back in time for the summer solstice?"

"Soon is all I can say," said Mr Bodkin. "There are still certain formalities that have to be completed."

He began to usher them towards the cold white corridor. Tom took one last look at the amazing underground workshop with its computer whizz-kids and Coca-cola cans and X-ray lasers, and then they were back in the silent underground tunnel. There, by some miracle, was Nigel's transit van, waiting for them in a parking bay. And there was Captain Snowball, back again without a word of explanation, standing beside it with an inscrutable expression on his face. "I think you'll find everything shipshape and Bristol fashion," he said, shaking the three of them firmly by the hand.

"Remember," Mr Bodkin wagged a thin grey finger, "you've signed the Official Secrets Act. Not a word to anyone, now." He turned to Tom, and put out his hand. "Well, young man, I've kept my part of the bargain, it's up to you to keep yours. The tape, please."

Tom felt strangely powerful as he fiddled with the straps on his satchel and took out the spool. "There you are," he said, feeling a bit like a hero in a Western. "After all, a deal is a deal."

"Indeed," said Mr Bodkin, taking the tape with a chilly smile. "Not a word to anyone, now. We have ways of finding out," he added grimly.

They all nodded, and climbed into the front seat of Suzanne. "If you drive straight on," said Captain Snowball, "you'll come out by what we call the Back Door."

Nigel turned on the engine and soon the van was rattling down the smooth grey tarmac under the phosphorescent orange lights of the tunnel.

"I wonder where this Back Door actually is," said Tom.

Nigel looked at his watch. "It will be dark now, so perhaps we won't recognise where we are."

Ahead they could see the black dot that was the end of the tunnel. They stopped at two checkpoints, but the security men had been warned and they went through without difficulty. And then suddenly they were outside and off the tarmac, bumping along a farm track.

They peered out through the windscreen. "I don't believe it," said Nigel, amazement in his voice. "I just don't – " He stopped the van.

"What?" said Tom and Harry almost with one voice.

"Look," said Nigel, opening the door and jumping out. "Look around you."

They were back at the radio observatory. There was the hill they'd just been under. There, behind them, was the smoke from the cement factory. And here, in a long silent line, mysterious and motionless as ever, were the seven satellite saucers staring up at the night sky. And overhead, millions of light years away, were tens of thousands of glittering stars.

Nigel was incredibly excited. "But of course," he was saying. "The X-ray laser had to be operated from a tracking station. And here it is. Why did I never put two and two together? Well, I suppose they didn't want me to. You never see what's under your nose . . ." He burbled on to himself in a language they could only half understand.

108

Harry gave Tom a gentle prod with her finger. "So I was right after all. Your dad *was* underground here," she whispered triumphantly.

But Tom was not bothered by Harry's boasting any more. He was looking up into the rich jewelled blackness with tears in his eyes and thanking the stars for leading him to his dad in the end. *I've done it*, he thought. *I've got my Dad back all on my own*. He looked at Harry and Nigel. *Well – with a little help from my friends*.

—— Chapter Fifteen ——

A HAPPY ENDING

Now that he knew about his dad's secret, it was funny being back at home again with his mother. He knew she was still basically in the dark. Half of him was dying to say, "Hey Mum, cheer up, Dad's coming home soon." But he'd promised to keep a secret and anyway how soon was soon? It could be another week. Maybe more. So he kept quiet. Which for him was very.

"I do hope you aren't in trouble again," she said as they watched Suzanne's tail-lights, with Nigel at the wheel, weave erratically down the road. "What do you mean, Mum?" It would be a big mistake to start telling her about what *really* went on inside the cement factory.

"I've had that Captain Snowball round here asking lots of questions about you."

So that was where he'd disappeared to!

"What sort of questions, Mum?"

It turned out that old Snowball had given her a real

torture-chamber job. Where was his school? Who were his friends and what were his school reports like? Who was Harriet? "He insisted on seeing your room."

"Oh – no!"

"Perhaps that will teach you to keep it tidier," she said, smiling. "He was very interested in your model ships."

Tom suddenly had a horrible thought. What if Snowball found the car number he'd given to Harry? Nervously, he asked if Captain Snowball had gone to the farm.

"I've no idea. You'll have to ask Harry."

Crikey! thought Tom. Once you'd signed the Official Secrets Act it was probably a torture-chamber offence to write down government car numbers.

So, as soon as possible after school the next day, he went to see Harry to talk things over. He had to find out if Captain Snowball had been there too. This time his mother made no fuss and there was no mention of phoning Mrs Bell.

"I won't be long," he said, half-expecting some Colditz-type interrogation.

"That's fine," said his mother. He could hardly believe his ears. *Things are getting better all the time.*

He walked across the fields, whistling. The village was behind him, and behind the village the chimneys of the cement factory were sending columns of laser-dust into the vast summer sky. What happened under the hill was *his* secret. It gave him a thrill to think that he and Harry could always look at it in a different way from ordinary people. He supposed that was what Nigel meant by "the inside story" – a nice warm feeling inside.

111

The footpath ran between high yellow corn now. At the corner of one field was a pill-box. Weeds had grown high against the entrance. The concrete was crumbling. The machine-gun slits were choked with stinging nettles. Whenever he went past he tried to imagine what it must have been like during the war. His dad had been his age in those days. There were faded family photographs of him in a school blazer standing next to the Mekon in army uniform. The Mekon had stories of German planes and bombs. He had fought with a general called Monty. It all seemed a long time ago. Perhaps Monty had inspected this pill-box. He would have come by helicopter, of course, except they probably didn't have helicopters in those days. Perhaps he came on a horse.

"Good morning men" – Monty would say, saluting.

"Good morning, sir" – the Mekon, of course, was in charge of his platoon.

"Shoot any Germans, today, chaps?" – Monty would ask.

"We're doing our best, sir."

"Carry on, men. You're doing a grand job."

And then Monty would have clattered away in his helicopter, or on his horse, or whatever, to fight the Germans somewhere else. Tom knew that in those days the Germans were on the Other Side. Mr Bodkin's words came into his head: "*We all know who's on the Other Side*." The trouble was, the Other Side kept on changing. It seemed odd to be fighting Germans. Tom had watched their football teams on TV. And there was a German boy called Klaus at his school who seemed fairly okay to him.

Now here he was at Harry's farm. She was grooming

Neddy in the yard. "Hello, fatso." She seemed quite pleased to see him. "What did your mum say?"

"Captain Snowball asked her a lot of questions while we were – well, you know where." He asked Harry if Snowball had been to the farm as well. Harry said no, she didn't think so.

"Do you still have that piece of paper I gave you with his car number on it?"

"Of course," said Harry. "It's in a very safe place."

"Where's that?"

"My knickers, stupid."

Tom was not embarrassed. "I think we should get rid of it in case he starts asking any more questions."

"That's easy." She put her hand into her jeans, fumbled about for a moment, and produced the scrap of paper. The day the black BMW first came to the house seemed a long time ago. "Here you are, Neddy," she said, and fed it to the llama, who munched it with obvious satisfaction.

Harry wanted to know if Tom believed what Mr Bodkin had said about his dad. "I bet you he doesn't come back after all," she said.

"Bet you he does."

So they had a bet on it.

Once upon a time Tom would not have trusted Harry with a bet. She simply could not be relied on to play fair. But now, as he watched her cleaning the llama's soft muddy feet, he realised that thanks to everything they had gone through together, he was looking at her in a different way from before. There was a good chance she wouldn't cheat him. She was, of course, still a bit of a mystery. She still didn't seem to be very interested in what he had to tell her about

113

lasers, Saturn, rockets and silicon chips. And he couldn't understand why she preferred Nigel to him. And this llama business was beyond him, really. *Why does she spend so much time with stupid animals?* He said out loud:

"Do you think that Neddy appreciates what you do for him?"

"Of course he does. It's just that he doesn't always show it, you see. He's not a demonstrative animal."

Actually, today she seemed a lot less keen on the llama than usual. And a lot more jumpy. It wasn't calming her down as it used to. Everything seemed to be a bit of a bore. *Perhaps she's missing Nigel?* Well, it was easy to find out. He casually mentioned something about Nigel and the cement factory. At once Harry perked up.

That's it, she's in love with Nigel. How boring! It was dreadfully confusing to feel so jealous of someone who was basically his best friend.

He simply couldn't resist asking if she preferred Nigel to Neddy.

Luckily for Tom the telephone rang in the farmhouse and Mrs Bell came out into the yard before Harry could attack him with her pitchfork.

"What does the old scumbag want now?" said Harry, slamming the fork on to a pile of manure and stamping off towards her aunt.

But it was for Tom. "It's your mother," said Mrs Bell.

Tom picked up the phone as if it weighed a ton. "Hello, Mum," he said wearily. *Same old story. She wants me back as soon as possible.*

"I've got to go home for tea," he told Harry, "See

114

you tomorrow." But Harry was still pretending to be upset. Tomorrow he would have to make it up to her somehow. She was too much of an essential friend to have her cross with him for long.

He went back across the flatlands to the village. *Perhaps my dad will be back soon. But how soon is soon? Everything is relative.*

He was thinking about everything that had happened when he realised he was nearly home, passing Mrs Grant's front door. He could hear someone inside her garage, rattling bottles. He tiptoed closer. There she was, her enormous bum sticking up in the air, bent over a box in the corner. It was obviously a secret supply of cigarettes or sherry. *I bet she's drunk as usual.* He looked round. There was no one in sight. It was now or never. *Silly old cow.* He reached up and gave the garage door a yank. Down it crashed. There were muffled shouts from within, but Tom did not turn back. He strolled on in the afternoon sunshine feeling, well, feeling extraordinarily satisfied.

He reached the stile, crossed the orchard and began climbing over the fence into their garden as usual. Then he stopped. He could hear a man's voice as well as his mother's. And laughter. And even Sarah didn't seem to be crying. He scrambled hurriedly over, stumbling slightly. Now he was running up the lawn. The man's voice said:

"Hello there, Tom."

It *was* his dad. Not a stand-in, or a dummy, or even Nigel.

"But – " He wanted to say that he wasn't expected yet, that soon wasn't this soon: he wanted to talk about the secrets under the hill, the X-ray lasers, and thousands of other things besides. Then he realised: *This is his inside story too.* And when his dad, who had the baby on his knee, just winked, he knew that they could talk everything over later on.

Cool, he said to himself, *stay cool.*

His mum and his dad were sitting in deck chairs, holding hands, looking very happy.

"Didn't I tell you he'd come back in the end?" said his mother.

Of course he didn't blame her for pretending that everything had been okay. Actually, he rather admired her for putting up such a good show. One day he'd have to explain to her how he'd done it all himself, but now was not the time. She was still talking. "Oh – and Sarah's just taken her first step. What a clever girl!"

While his mother went on about his sister's amazing achievements, Tom went up to his dad and pinched him on the nose just to make sure. "Hi, Dad," he said, extra-cool. "So did you have a good time?"

"I'll tell you about it sometime," said his father, and winked again. Tom looked at him very carefully. Yes, both ears were fine. So Harry was wrong about that, anyway. *What does she know?* Here was his dad at last: *the world is a banana.*

Super cool, thought Tom. "You're just in time for the solstice," he said. He couldn't show it, of course, but he was happier than a total eclipse. *I did it! I've got my dad back. I really have.* It was hard to be super super-cool. Midsummer's Day was the day after tomorrow. He knew that the time would soon come when they would talk it all over, together, by the light of the stars.